MW00915882

LEIA STONE

THE RUTHLESS FAE KING

TRIGGER WARNING

Non-consensual sex and kidnapping are present in this book. They are not presented in a graphic or overly detailed way.

1

"I won't do it, Father!" I screamed.

"Do you want the entire realm to be plunged into winter? Or our crops to fail?" my father yelled back. "When the winter king asks for your daughter's hand in marriage, you don't say no!"

I was so angry I was shaking. I'd never been this mad at my father in my entire life. I loved him, adored him, worshipped the ground he walked on, but I would not relent to marrying that monster.

"Well, that's exactly what I'm going to say when he gets here. NO!" I shouted, and wind picked up inside the house, causing the papers on my father's desk to fly into the air and form a funnel.

He sighed, as if he were used to my outbursts, but that wasn't fair. I didn't have them that often, only when being forced to be married off to a heartless jackass!

"Daddy..." I softened my voice and the wind died down immediately, bringing the papers to a slow descent to the floor. "I love you. I respect your decision-making. But I will not under *any* circumstances marry Lucien Thorne. *Ever.*"

My father looked up at me with sadness in his eyes and I knew then that it was already done. Arranged marriages were common among royalty, and I always knew as the princess of Fall I would one day be called on by a royal suitor, but Lucien, the winter king?

It was unthinkable.

"No." A strangled cry came from my lips and my father could no longer meet my gaze.

"I'm sorry, Madelynn. There's nothing that can be done," he said. And that was that.

My fate was sealed to the most vile man in all of Thorngate. Lucien had only been king for six winters and yet I had over a dozen stories of his evil doings. He once froze the entire Summer crop when they protested his raise in taxes. I also heard that he took the tongue of his favorite chef for serving him bland food.

He hated flowers, so he had them all destroyed for miles around his palace. He was dead inside. *Evil.* Ever since his father abdicated the throne to him on his sixteenth birthday, there had been nothing but rumors of his darkness.

"What if he beats me?" I tried to reason with my father. "You've heard the rumors, Daddy. He's unkind."

My father looked stricken. "He would not hit his wife." He didn't sound sure though.

Maker help me.

My father was kind, *too* kind, and always trying to please others. Now I was going to have to deal with this myself. I would have to be strong so that King Thorne knew I was not the type of woman to be crossed.

"When does he arrive?" I asked through gritted teeth.

"Later this afternoon." My father's voice was small.

"Today!" I bellowed, and the wind was back, blowing through the open window and swirling around me. My powers were the strongest seen in generations, and I knew that's why the king had chosen me. I'd never met Lucien Thorne as an adult. We Fall Court fae stuck to ourselves mostly. I'd briefly seen him as a young boy back when his mother was still alive, but I must have been six winters old and he only eight or so. I barely remembered that. He'd handed me a sunflower and told me my dress was pretty. A sweet boy—before the darkness took him over.

I stormed from my father's office, taking the wind spiral with me.

How dare my father tell me hours before the king was to arrive! It gave me no time to find a way out of this arrangement. And maybe that's what he wanted.

The palace staff hugged the walls as I passed, my wind blowing their dresses left and right. I needed to go outside and blow off some of this anger before I collapsed the entire house.

Bursting out the back doors, I ran past the gardens towards the meadow I often went to when I wanted to use my power without destroying anything.

Once in the safety of nature, I let loose. I sucked in a huge lungful of air and the wind pressed in on me like an old friend. The grass bowed, dust kicked up, and the sun darkened as my little wind tunnel grew stronger.

Maybe the king was on his way right now. It was late afternoon and he might be en route. If I sent this little windstorm his way, it might blow his horses off track and he could be injured, delaying the engagement...

I shook myself from those dark thoughts, knowing such a thing would be traced back to me.

Balling my hands into fists, I looked up at the sky,

into the eye of the storm I'd created, and let loose with an agonizing scream, aiming it at the sun as if it was his fault I was upset.

All at once the wind died out and I was calm again. Unleashing my power would not help me. I needed to keep a level head if I was going to find a way out of this.

"Your father told you?" My mother's voice sounded behind me and I spun on her like a snake ready to strike.

"Mother, how could you?" I whimpered. My father was the leader of this court, it was his duty to make such an arrangement, but my mother? She gave me no warning.

Her eyes filled with tears. "The winter king can be very convincing," was all she said.

I scoffed, stepping closer to her. She had the same bright red hair as I did, and today we both wore lime green dresses without knowing the other would be doing it. We often did this and I liked it. I'd felt a closeness with my mother my entire life, but now I just felt betrayed.

"Mother, he's awful," I pleaded.

She sighed. "Don't say that. He was a boy who lost his mother and he... acted out."

She was defending him?

"He lost his mother *six* years ago," I growled. "What's his excuse now?"

His mother died in a tragic accident. She was riding with young Lucien Thorne when she was bucked off her horse. She fell on her neck and it snapped, killing her instantly. Because they were on an innocent horseback ride, there had been no healing elf present. I did feel bad that a young boy had to see his mother die like that, but it was no excuse for some of the stories I'd heard about him.

"Mother, he eats raw meat. He's killed with his bare hands. Not to mention what he did with the Great Freeze. He's a monster."

My mother sighed. "We don't know if *all* of those stories are true." She didn't sound too sure about that.

"Is it the dowry he's paying? Because I can raise my own money and pay you and Daddy back—"

My mother cut me off with the shake of her head. "No, honey, it's law. When the reigning king asks for a royal's hand in marriage, it cannot be refused."

I frowned.

Law? A stupid little legal edict was standing in the way of my freedom? It wasn't that I was against duty, or marriage. My parents were arranged and had a wonderful marriage. I knew my day would come soon. I was just against the idea of *him*.

"Why does he want me?" I crossed my arms and tipped my chin up. "I'm from Fall Court. Duchess Dunia of Winter would be a *much* better match. They

6

grew up together, she knows him. Their offspring would be better suited."

My mother sighed, stepping forward, and grasped my hands in hers. "He has heard of your power and beauty. He wants *you*, Madelynn, to be his wife and the mother of his children. Your son could be future king."

My heart sank. My power and beauty were not things I thought would one day seal my fate to an evil prick, but here we were.

"I'm sorry, Mother. I can't. Anyone but him. Help me say no. Say I am betrothed to another, or—"

"Madelynn! That would embarrass your father and our entire court. You've already been promised." She looked at me like I'd grown two heads. Her perfect eldest daughter. Most powerful with wind magic. Top marks in school. Never stepped a toe out of line. Sure, I was independent and headstrong, but I never disobeyed my parents, or a royal edict... until now.

"I'll see you later, Mother," I said cryptically, and then ran to the horse barn to find my mare.

There was no way in Hades I was marrying Lucien Thorne.

I RODE INTO TOWN ALONE, disguised under the hood of my cloak until I came to one of my favorite courtier's houses, Maxwell Blane. He was handsome, rich, funny, and a total lothario. It would be perfect for what I was about to ask.

I knocked on his door hurriedly, as the street beyond his house in town was bustling and I didn't want any rumors. I'd never been alone in another man's presence without a chaperone, but I didn't want a witness for what I was about to ask of him.

When his housemaid opened the door, I slipped inside without being asked to do so.

She squeaked in shock, backing up, then I pulled off my cloak. "Sorry for the intrusion, Margaret."

"Oh, Princess Madelynn." She bowed, seemingly relieved that she knew who was barging into her home.

My lady-in-waiting, Piper, and I came to Maxwell's house once a week for one of his famous cocktail parties. He was the courtier to know, and put on the most entertaining parties I'd ever been to. There was singing, games, and drinking. I didn't drink of course, it wouldn't be proper but I played the games and we always had a wonderful time.

"Is Maxwell around? I have an urgent issue."

She nodded. "Right this way. He's in the study." She looked behind me at the door as if nonverbally asking where my chaperone was. I said nothing, only letting the heat of my cheeks speak for me. Without a word, she took the hint and asked for my cloak.

Maxwell's parents came from old money, and when they died in a boating accident they left him everything. He was a spoiled brat and a dear friend. I knew he would help me with my request.

She walked me down the hallway. We came upon an open door and the maid knocked on the casing. "Sir, Princess Madelynn is here."

His face lit up when he saw me. "What an honor. Come in, darling."

Darling. Beautiful. Honey. He never addressed a woman without something sweet at the end. He'd bedded half the court, I was sure of it.

The maid left us. Normally, she would stay to make sure my reputation was intact, but I think she had gathered this was going to be a private conversation.

I shut the door behind me and then turned to face him.

He wore a red silk smoking jacket and held a lit cigar along with a cup of coffee, a large diamond ring on his pinky. He was twenty-three years old. The town gossiped about his single status weekly but he'd informed me once that he had no intentions of getting married. Ever.

Out of politeness he extinguished his cigar and

stood to kiss my cheek. I accepted the kiss and kissed him back in the affectionate way I would a brother or beloved uncle. I'd never been attracted to Maxwell. He was handsome, but his flagrant flirting and the ease at which he bedded women turned me off. Now I realized it was exactly what I needed.

"To what do I owe this secret pleasure?" He beamed at me, looking at the closed door and my lack of chaperone as he sat back down in his chair.

I took a shaky breath and leveled my gaze on his. "My father has just betrothed me to Lucien Thorne."

His coffee cup stilled on his lips and he set it back down. "Oh dear, that man has a nasty reputation. But you will be queen, so that's a plus."

I shook my head. "I obviously can't marry him, Max. You have to help me."

Maxwell had long, dark-blond hair, ice-blue eyes, and his skin was softer than mine. Sometimes I studied his face wondering how he could be so... beautiful. I did this now while he considered my fate.

He nodded. "I see. I can give you money, you can pay your father the dowry—"

I held up my hand and interrupted him. "My mother said he won't take it. It's not about the money, it's about reputation."

Maxwell chewed his lip. "Well, you could take some money from me and run away."

I scoffed. "And leave my family? My home?"

He shrugged. "I don't know any other option, Madelynn. He's the winter king," he said, and took a sip of his coffee.

I tapped my fingers nervously on my legs, my cheeks going red with embarrassment. "As you know, there is a purity test before marrying the king. I was wondering if you could help me... fail it."

His coffee spurted out of his mouth and in my direction. I barely had time to move before it covered the seat behind me.

His mouth was agape and I winced.

"Are you trying to get me killed?" he exclaimed. "Your father would kill me, then your mother, and then the king. I'd be thrice dead!"

"I'm desperate!" I sobbed. "He's a monster. You know this."

His gaze traveled down my body, then he reached up and bit one of his knuckles before pulling it from his mouth. "I will admit I've thought of bedding you, Madelynn, but you're royalty and I don't do drama." Maxwell looked at me with pity. "I can offer money that does not need repayment, but it's all I can do."

It was a nice offer, but I wasn't leaving my family and my home.

I frowned. "Max, I don't want to marry him."

Reaching across the desk, he grasped my hand in

his. "Be the strong, bold, and independent woman I know you to be and maybe he will reject you."

I laughed, but then thought maybe that was a decent idea. If I was nasty enough to him, he would realize my beauty and power were no consolation for the kind of nightmarish woman I could be.

"That's brilliant. Thanks, Max."

He took one more longing look at me and waved me off. "Go, before I change my mind."

I wished him farewell and then grabbed my cloak from his maidservant. When I got to the front door and flung it open, my mother was leaning against my horse.

Hades.

That woman knew me too well. I tried to act calm, like I wasn't just caught doing something I shouldn't.

My mother shot me a glare as I approached. "Going off to the local seducer without a chaperone? You wouldn't be trying to tarnish your reputation, now would you, daughter?"

I huffed. "He wouldn't have me."

"Madelynn!" my mother scolded, reaching out to whack me on the back of the head for good measure. "Your father has betrothed you to the winter king, the ruler of all fae. You could do no better."

My mother and father seemed to have blocked out all of the horror stories of Lucien Thorne.

"You gave me no time to prepare for this," I

growled, suddenly feeling ashamed with what I'd just done. If word got around that I was alone in Maxwell's house without a chaperone, I would have *no* marriage prospects from *any* man.

My mom rested a hand on my shoulder and looked me in the eye. "Because we know you too well." She eyed Maxwell's house as if to make a point. "Listen, honey, we raised you to be a leader," my mother said. "At King Thorne's side, you can make a difference. As his wife and our queen, you will influence law and carry out rulings. You can give back to your community and even talk him down from war. A woman has an important place beside a king."

Her words touched me, touched the place inside of me that wanted to sacrifice my happiness for that of my people. I had naïvely assumed I could have both happiness and duty, but now I knew that not to be true.

I sighed in resignation. "If he hurts me, I'll kill him. Consequences be dammed."

My mother flinched as if I'd slapped her. "If he hurts you, *I'll* kill him."

Her shock at my mention of him being abusive made me wonder if I was being too harsh on the winter king. But the stories I'd heard—that he once dragged a courtier through the town behind a horse—they were all dark and brutal, and told the tale of an unhinged king who I wanted *nothing* to do with.

Tears suddenly filled my vision and a gust of wind passed over us, picking up my hair. "I'm going to miss you."

I barely got the words out when my mother pulled me into a hug.

THE WINTER KING would be here any minute. After we negotiated my dowry, he would parade me around Fall Court like a prized hog. We would announce our engagement publicly and then go on a tour of the four courts, inviting each one to our upcoming wedding. And all of this was before I'd even met the man or agreed to it.

In the end, I relented to my father's begging and my mother's tears.

I was the most powerful princess in all the realm, and the king wanted powerful heirs, so it was an obvious pairing.

A part of me sort of always knew this day would come. I'd just hoped he'd marry a woman of royal lineage from his own court and leave me alone.

I didn't want to leave Fall. Orange leaves, crisp cool air, the scent of change. I'd grown up in my father's kingdom my entire life. We were one of the most prosperous of Thorngate, growing half the food for the realm, and even selling excess to Embergate.

I sat in my room as my beloved lady-in-waiting, Piper, finished curling my hair, and I gasped at the sudden realization that I would no longer have her company. I was nineteen winters old and she was twenty. We practically grew up together. Her mother served as my mother's lady-in-waiting and she'd become my best friend.

We'd been quiet since we both heard the news. I wasn't sure she knew what to think or say to me. Marrying the winter king was more of a curse than a blessing, so congratulations were not in order.

"What's wrong?" she asked me finally.

Unshed tears filled my eyes as I looked up at her. "I just realized I would be losing you. I could never ask you to leave your family and follow me to the frozen Hades of Winter Court."

Piper smiled. I loved that smile. She had two crooked teeth in front that pressed onto her bottom lip like fangs.

"Oh, Maddie, I would never leave you to marry that bastard alone. I've already asked your father to be dismissed from Fall Court. I'm going to Winter with you."

Tears lined my eyes and I pulled her in for a hug. "I don't deserve you," I told her.

I released her and she nodded, her long brown hair shaking around her shoulders. "That's true. And I hear the winter king is richer than your father, so maybe I should ask for a raise..."

I grinned, loving that Piper knew how to get me out of my rotten mood.

There was a knock at the door and I stood, squaring my shoulders and tipping my chin high.

It was time. He was here.

As I strode towards the door, Piper caught my wrist. I turned to look at her and there was a fire in her eyes. "Remember your worth, Madelynn Windstrong. You have a lot to offer. I don't care if he is king. You're worth more than a bag of gold."

My heart pinched, and I thanked the Maker for such a loyal friend. Squeezing her hand, I nodded and then opened the door to find my mother waiting for me. The dowry negotiation was always done in person after the male suitor met the prospective wife. He would want to make sure I looked as pretty as he had heard, or last seen, and that I was as powerful as rumor stated. The prettier and more powerful, the more money and land my father could ask for.

Because I would be giving him power in his kingship and future heirs, he would pay my father for the right to marry me. It was a practice as old as time in our culture, one that if I stopped to think about felt a little offensive, but was necessary to keep our court funded. My father didn't ask for many taxes from the people, and fifty percent of what we got we had to give to the ruling monarch, the winter king.

"You look beautiful, dear," my mother said, and extended her arm so that I could hook mine into hers.

"Thank you." I took her arm and then looked back at Piper, who gave me a thumbs-up.

I loved her for saying she would go with me. Truthfully, I wasn't sure I would be able to survive in Winter without at least one friend.

As my mother and I traversed the hallways of my family home, I felt reality settle in. I couldn't believe I was doing this. The man who was rumored to have killed a servant for not making his bed correctly was about to be my husband.

Could I marry a man who would make me miserable for the rest of my life just to honor my duty and make my family happy? Was duty above happiness?

Unfortunately for me, it was.

"Maddie!" My little sister's voice came from behind me and my entire body went rigid. If I saw her right now I would fall into a puddle of tears. I couldn't imagine leaving Libby.

"She doesn't know yet," my mother whispered, and relief rushed through me.

I spun, plastering on a fake smile, and let her rush into my arms.

"I got top marks in archery! Master Bellman says I'm as good as the elves!" she shouted excitedly.

I grinned, smoothing her frizzed red hair with my palms. She had mine and our mother's red hair coloring but my father's texture. She looked like a wild lion half the time. "I imagine you are."

"You look pretty." She took in my gold embroidered dress and fancy hair and makeup.

"Thank you. I have... a meeting, so I will come by after and talk with you, okay?" Saying goodbye to her would kill me. I couldn't even think of it right now.

"'kay!" she shouted, and then ran to our mother to hug her before she was bouncing off down the hall to her room with her nanny running behind her.

I shared a heartbreaking look with my mother but said nothing.

Libby and I had a special relationship. I'd watched as my mother had cruelly gone through seven miscarriages before Libby was born eight years ago. When she came into our lives, it was the breath of fresh air we all needed. She kept things fun and light in the palace. She was the joy in my mother's heart after so much sorrow.

When we reached the door, I looked at my mother to hit her with the truth. If I was going to marry this man with the heinous reputation he had, I wanted to have control over certain things.

"I want to negotiate my own dowry," I told her boldly.

She almost choked on her own spit, coughing and clearing her throat. "Honey, that's not done. It's between King Thorne and your father."

I tipped my chin high. "If I'm going to be sold to a monster, I will state the price I am worth, no one else."

My mother's cheeks burned with shame and I felt awful for saying it that way. Her curt nod was all I needed before I opened the door.

When my gaze fell on Lucien Thorne laughing near the fireplace with my father, I knew I was in trouble.

I'd built up a deep hatred for this man. The things he'd done were inexcusable, and yet when my gaze fell on him, I couldn't help the tightening of my stomach and the warm wash of pleasure that rushed through me.

He was the most attractive man I'd ever seen. I faltered as he turned to look at me.

Oh, Maker, have mercy.

Lucien Thorne was nothing like the boyish paintings hanging in meeting halls. The man before me was chiseled perfection: steely gray eyes, a sharp nose and strong jaw. His lips were pursed and thick. He wore the hairstyle of royal warriors, his long black tresses shaved at the sides and then pulled into a ponytail, braided at the very edges. His charcoal-gray tunic hugged his muscular body, leaving little to the imagination. I didn't know what I was expecting, but not this, not to feel attracted to the man I hated. It threw me for a second, as the king and I just stood there and stared at each other. His gaze raked over me slowly and I felt my breath hitch.

He was evil incarnate, and yet wrapped in the most delicious package I'd ever seen. I wasn't sure I could resist whatever he would offer as a dowry.

I can't marry this man.

Shaking myself, I pulled out of whatever spell he'd cast over me and remembered his reputation.

"My king..." I curtsied the least amount possible to still be considered polite and then stepped closer to greet him.

My mother curtsied next to me, deeply and overly respectful.

He watched me like an animal tracking prey, and I swallowed hard.

"Madelynn Windstrong, you are far more beautiful than the songs written about you," he stated, and stepped forward, reaching for my hand. I offered it to him and he kissed it lightly, a zap of cold traveling up my arm as he did.

A charmer too. Great.

I gave him a curt smile. He then kissed my mother's hand as well. Because he was so handsome, I took this time to remind myself of every horrible story I'd heard of him, and then turned to my father.

"I've spoken to Mother about wanting to negotiate my dowry myself and she agrees," I told him right in front of the king.

My father made a choking sound and my gaze flicked to the king to see what he would say or do, but he just watched me with amusement. His hands were clasped behind his back calmly and his eyes crinkled as he assessed me.

"That's not done. It's men's work," my father said, and then gave a nervous peal of laughter before looking at the king. "I'm sorry, my lord, I think I raised her to be a little *too* independent and headstrong."

The king was still watching me, his steel gray eyes boring into mine. "I think I'd pay extra for independent and headstrong."

His comment shocked me. What the Hades did *that* mean? Was he joking? I didn't like it if he was.

My father didn't even know what to do with that, so he remained silent.

"I would be happy to negotiate your dowry with you, Madelynn," the king said to me, and I gulped.

Saying I wanted to negotiate my own payment was one thing, doing it was another.

I hadn't actually expected him to accept. I'd hoped he would have seen the move as too pushy and domineering and called the entire thing off.

I looked to my father and mother, knowing that if I were about to actually agree to marry this man I needed to have a private conversation with him first.

"Mother, Father, if you will excuse us, I need to speak with King Thorne alone before I can agree to marry him."

A panicked look flashed across my father's face. He knew me too well, and was probably imagining all of the horrible things I would say or do.

"You cannot be alone with an unmarried man. It's not proper," my mother reminded me, giving a nervous laugh.

I nodded. "Go fetch Piper. She can chaperone."

My father was frozen by the fireplace as if unsure he could break protocol and allow this. We all stared at the king for guidance, but the king appeared to be perfectly calm and enjoying himself. He leaned against the brick wall of the drawing room casually.

"I look forward to our private chat," he stated to me.

My mother scurried off then to look for Piper, and I started to grow uneasy with the winter king's accommodating personality. Surely the monstrous king I had heard of would forbid such a thing. A woman negotiating her own dowry was unheard of, yet he looked as if this amused him, which infuriated me.

What was he playing at? It seemed if I'd hoped to turn him off with this behavior, I was mistaken.

A moment later my mother appeared with Piper, who bowed deeply to the king and then stood in the far corner of the room to be a silent spectator.

My father cleared his throat, obviously out of his element.

"You may leave us," I told my father. My mother was already standing in the doorway.

My father looked to the king, who nodded, and then my parents reluctantly left. As soon as the door shut, I stepped closer to Lucien Thorne. I decided to be as honest as possible so that he knew where I was coming from.

"I've heard the stories about you," I told him. "You're a cruel man who is unkind to staff members, and severely punishes people for the smallest infraction. I would be lying if I said I was excited to be your betrothed."

There, I'd done it. I was completely honest to him, and allowed there to be no pretenses between us that I was going to be some doting wife who was in love with him. It was a bold thing to say to a king, and I awaited his angry response.

Instead, the bastard just smiled at my verbal account of his reputation.

I crossed my arms and pinned him with a glare. "And *furthermore*, I'm not interested in giving you children right away, so you will have to wait until I am ready."

His gaze went half lidded and he licked his lips as if imagining having children with me.

Heat traveled to my cheeks and I flushed. "And I will not bed you unless we are making a child. You can take a mistress, or a whore, I don't care." I tipped my chin high, then a bark of laughter erupted from his throat.

The sound shook me. It was deep and gravelly and filled the entire room.

"Are you laughing at me?" My hands balled into fists and a light gust of wind filled the drawing room, causing the fire in the hearth to increase its flame.

A sudden flurry of snow drifted into the hearth, down the chimney and dropped onto the fire, causing it to crackle.

Was he displaying his power because I had? What the Hades was this? Were we in some sort of showdown?

He just watched me, smiling and seemingly entertained as I wrestled with all of my emotions.

Reaching up, he grabbed his heart. "I think I just fell in love."

I rolled my eyes, groaning as the wind died out in an instant. Was this man going to be an insufferable charmer the entire time?

"I tell you that I think you are a horrible person and you fall in love with me?" I asked. "You sound unstable."

He stepped forward quickly, causing my heart to quicken as he suddenly strode to within two inches of me. "I'm not known for being stable, am I?" he whispered, his warm breath washing over me.

Holy Maker.

I stepped back a pace, looking towards Piper in panic, but she was statue-still, an observer. She played the role well when she needed to, but we would no doubt be talking about this for days when we were alone.

He took another step, closing the distance I had just gained, and lowered his voice. "I have a confession to make," he murmured.

My heart was in my throat and I swallowed hard. "What?" I breathed.

Why did he have to be so handsome?

He looked down at my lips, and then at my throat

25

before finally meeting my eyes. "I saw you in the meadow by your house last full moon. I was traveling with some of my soldiers in the woods. We were searching for a lost hunting dog. You were dancing in the garden with your sister and..." He took in a deep breath, reaching out to catch a lock of my red hair. "I thought you were the most beautiful woman I'd ever seen. I knew then I had to have you."

It was as if all of the air had been sucked from the room. I couldn't breathe. What was happening? The evil king was... complimenting me?

"Name your price, Madelynn Windstrong, because there isn't a piece of gold in the realm I wouldn't pay to be able to wake up next to you each morning." He smiled sweetly then and I had to swallow a whimper. It was the sweetest thing a man had ever said to me and... it was coming from the bastard who'd caused my family so much pain in the past. I didn't know what to say or feel. I was... at odds with myself. What I had initially assumed were a charmer's flirtations had quickly become a serious confession.

"When you first became king and you brought the Great Freeze across the entire land, my grandmother died," I blurted out.

A darkness cast over his face and I almost regretted saying it. I was already getting used to his smile.

I was now staring at a man devoid of all emotion. He'd retreated somewhere, a place I couldn't follow, a place I didn't want to follow.

"I'm sorry I killed her," he stated. "Others too. Thirty-seven people died in Summer Court that night. Twelve in Spring. They weren't prepared for that kind of cold."

My brows knotted together as he confessed the horrible things he'd done without an ounce of emotion.

"You admit it?" We'd never gotten an apology or explanation. Just an extreme cold that ripped across the land and the next day it was back to normal.

"I do." He stood tall, his back erect and his chin up, his smile gone. "My powers are tied to my emotions. Same as yours. I couldn't control them." He was speaking about a moment ago when I couldn't keep the wind from entering the room.

What kind of emotions did this man have that he would end up freezing the entire realm for a full day and night? I was thirteen at the time, and it had been one of the scariest nights of my life. The cold crept into the house like a shadow and lingered no matter how high we built the fire. I didn't sleep; my teeth chattered all night. I stood outside with Mother, pushing the frost back with our wind power. My grandmother came out to help us, but she was too old for that kind of exposure. She passed the next day. A weak heart, the healer had said, but we all knew what weakened her.

The Great Freeze.

Since he was being so open, I wanted to ask him what had happened that night to make him lose control, but I wasn't sure I wanted the answer. I didn't want to know what kind of man I was marrying. A scary man who could freeze me solid if I made him angry.

I didn't know what to say. This was supposed to be a dowry negotiation and it had somehow turned into something else.

The king stared at me then and there was something deep in his eyes that brought a pain to my heart. He looked... sad. Like maybe deep inside of him there was a desolate little boy who just wanted to be loved.

"I know arranged marriages are not ideal anymore, but they are tradition," King Thorne said. "That being said, if you do not want to tie your fate to mine, I can cancel the whole thing. I will tell your father we are simply not a good match. No harm will come to your reputation."

I frowned, my heart thudding into my throat. He was giving me an out? A seriousness descended onto the room and I warred with what I wanted before I'd met him, how I felt now, and what my mother and father expected of me.

"Honestly," the winter king said, "I feel like I should be asking *you* to pay a dowry to be married to this." He gestured up and down his body and laughter erupted from my chest.

He was funny.

Funny.

Charming.

Sweet.

Slightly unhinged. What could go wrong?

His offer to allow me to back out of the arrangement was noteworthy, but my father had already told the elders of the Fall Court. Not to mention the king rode up here with a full contingent of royal soldiers. Half the town probably already knew what was going on. If we were to cancel, rumor would spread and people would say that there was something wrong with me, that I was impure or too independent. This would tarnish any potential future suitors.

No, I had to do this now. My family's reputation was on the line. This would impact Libby's prospects as well. As much as I'd wanted him to back out before, now I saw the ripple effect that would have on my family.

"We can proceed with the arrangement." I smoothed my dress in a nervous gesture. "I just wanted you to know where I stood."

He nodded, assessing me coolly. "You don't want

children right away, will only bed me for children, and I can take a whore. Got it."

I winced when he said it like that, and then gave a nervous peal of laughter. "Okay, the whore comment was a little strong. I'm sorry. This is... a lot for me all at once. I was only told today."

He regarded me with a grin. "Does this mean you are taking away my promised whore?"

I reached out and slapped his shoulder like I would an old friend, forgetting for a second I was in the presence of the king. But he caught my hand, holding my fingers lightly, which caused my mind to race.

"I would never do that to you... take a whore, or a mistress, or anything in between," he promised, and my stomach flipped over itself.

He was so... not what I thought he would be.

"How much dowry did your father pay your mother's family?" I asked him, pulling my fingers from his and trying to get a feel for what was a good amount to ask for.

The mention of his deceased mother caused his face to fall a little before he regained composure. "A hundred gold coins, ten acres of land, and a dozen horses. But that was a simpler time." His voice was monotone, and I wondered if speaking of his mother after so long was something he didn't like to do.

A hundred gold coins was how much my father

made in a year, and King Thorne would be taking me from my father for life.

"I want a *thousand* gold coins," I told him, ready for him to whittle me down to five hundred.

"Done," he stated without missing a beat.

I froze, and then swallowed hard. He was awfully agreeable. "And I want my beloved lady-in-waiting to come as well." I nodded to Piper, who stood erect in the corner.

"Done," he said again.

My heart hammered in my chest. "Also, I think a hundred acres of farmable land for my people is a fair price for the two heirs I will give you."

The king looked my body up and down slowly, his gray eyes caressing my skin so that I could almost feel it. "I was hoping to have more children than that, especially since you stated you will only lie with me when making children."

Piper's snort-laugh came from the corner, and I turned over my shoulder to glare at her. Heat traveled up my cheeks and I knew that they probably resembled the color of my hair.

"The number of children can be discussed later." I fanned myself and stepped away from the fire.

"A hundred acres. Done," he said.

"As far as horses, we have twenty elders in Fall Court. I would like you to gift each one a new stallion. They do most of our farming and this will help—"

"Done," he interrupted me. "Anything else?"

I looked at him incredulously. That had been way easier than I thought. He was saying yes without hesitation. "Will I be able to see my family?" My voice broke as I thought of Libby.

"Of course." His lips pulled into a frown. "Whenever you like. They are welcome at Winter Court anytime. We have a lovely guest house I can have ready at a moment's notice."

I had planned to tell him that if he ever hurt me I would tear his body in two with the strongest wind imaginable, but now I felt that might be too unkind of an assessment. Had he done bad things in his past? *Yes* —he admitted to the Great Freeze. But there was something else there, a gentleness I couldn't describe, an eagerness to please, to be loved. It held me in confusion and tempered my anger towards him.

I knew that dowries were sealed with a handshake, so I stepped forward and extended my hand.

"I look forward to the upcoming nuptials and serving our people as queen," I told him.

He smiled then, taking my hand into a strong, firm grip and shaking it. "I look forward to spending the rest of my life with you, Madelynn. I hope I can make you happy."

I stopped breathing for the umpteenth time. The way he spoke was... so intense, so real. He leaned forward and pressed a small kiss to the top of my hand before gently dropping it, and I was almost sad to see it go. The winter king then crossed the room, tipping his head to Piper as he went. When his hand rested on the door handle, I called to him. "King Thorne!"

He turned back to look at me, and I met his steely gaze.

"I could have asked for more, couldn't I?"

The slow halfcocked grin that spread across his face made my knees go weak. *Good night*, he was handsome. "There is nothing I would have denied you."

He turned then and shut the door softly. Probably to go in search of my father and put all of this in writing.

I stood there stunned as Piper peeled herself away from the wall and stood before me.

"Do we still hate him?" she asked with a frown. "I'm so confused."

I shrugged. "What the Hades just happened?"

She chewed her bottom lip. "I kind of liked everything about him."

So did I.

So. Did. I.

While the king put everything in writing with my father and signed it, Piper and I were in the drawing room, reading and waiting for the purity test. I dreaded what came next. The healer would check to make sure I was indeed intact for my king. My mother told me it would feel awkward for a moment but would be over quickly.

The door opened suddenly and a male elvin healer walked in wearing a white healer's robe. King Thorne stepped in behind him. I hadn't expected a male healer. I shared a look with Piper and gulped, clenching my thighs at the thought of a strange man looking between my legs.

"I said *no*. I told you not to come," the winter king growled at the healer.

My father and mother had not yet returned and so I would have to navigate this myself.

The healer wore a typical white robe and carried a black healer's bag. "Your father has demanded it," the healer said.

The room was suddenly plunged into coldness as frigid temperatures coated my skin. "My father is no longer king," he barked at the healer. "The only man I want seeing her naked is me. If you touch her, I'll freeze your hand and break it off. Understood?"

I stiffened, and Piper moved protectively to my side.

This was the temper he was famous for. Freezing and breaking off your own healer's hand! It was insane. I was so confused by his behavior. Didn't he want to make sure I was pure? I didn't know what to think of this man. He was breaking all the rules.

"Just the written statement will suffice," King Thorne told him.

The healer's jaw tensed but he nodded, then he turned to face me. "Madelynn Windstrong, do you swear on the Maker that you are pure from sexual defilement?"

I swallowed hard, my cheeks heating. "I swear," I squeaked.

He handed me a piece of paper that said as much and I signed it with a shaking hand.

As the healer was leaving, my mother and father entered the room, both smiling. Clearly they were happy with the dowry I had secured.

"Is the purity check done already?" my mom asked, seeing the healer leaving.

"It is," the king said, not stating that I'd never been physically checked.

"Would you like to see a display of her power before it gets dark?" My father beamed. He was always so proud of my magical abilities. It was sweet.

King Thorne looked across the drawing room at me. "If Madelynn doesn't mind. I know we have to leave early in the morning for the engagement tour, so if you are tired I understand."

Piper and I shared a look. Why was he so considerate? Was this all an act? It didn't make sense. The selfish and angry winter king I heard rumors about was not the man who stood before me.

I stood, straightening my back. "I'm always down to show off a little," I exclaimed, to which my mother scoffed.

"She is rather humble, my lord, I promise," my mother told the king nervously.

"Not when it comes to her power," Piper said honestly, which got a chuckle from my father.

I glanced at the king to find him smirking at me. It was as if I brought him great delight with my rebellious, unladylike behavior.

We all stepped outside into the flat meadow surrounded by trees. A few of them were knocked over from the last time I'd displayed a tremendous amount of wind power.

I could feel the king standing at my back, and turned to see him a mere foot away, watching me with interest. My mother, father, and Piper, however, stood a good six feet away.

"You're going to want to stand back further, my lord," I told him.

His eyes glittered as if the thought that I could hurt him was asinine.

Taking my heed, he stepped back to where the others were waiting, then I drew in a deep breath. Calling the wind to me, it filtered through the trees, pulling leaves with it as it came. I started with a show of force, using the wind to pick up a fallen tree and lift the large log into the air, spinning it wildly.

The sounds of clapping came from behind me and I turned to see my mother, father, Piper and the winter king all cheering me on.

"Impressive!" King Thorne shouted.

Encouraged by the audience, I dropped the log and gathered more leaves, wanting to end the performance with a beautiful swirl of colors. Brown, orange, green, and bright yellow leaves ripped from the branches and joined the swirl of wind. A gasp of surprise came from behind me, from *right* behind me, and I knew it was the king. My mother and father had seen this dozens of times—they could do it too, on a smaller scale. Piper wouldn't be shocked either as she'd seen me do it often.

"You're incredible," King Thorne breathed, and then he was right beside me, his hands reaching out to mine. "May I?"

I didn't know what he meant, but it would be rude to deny the king, so I nodded. And that's when it began to snow. Not on us, or my parents, it was strictly controlled to the funnel. I watched as snowflakes dropped into my wind funnel and then were sucked into the swirling motion. The white flurry reminded me of a snowglobe toy I had when I was a child. Whenever I got angry I would shake it and watch the snow fall and it would soothe me. That was happening now. The snow and the bright leaves were in perfect sync, making a soothing spiral around the meadow. It was as if my magic and his were made for each other, and if I was honest, it was one of the most beautiful things I'd ever seen.

My parents and Piper started to clap and I dropped my hands, dissipating the wind tunnel.

"I'm famished," I told my mother, giving King Thorne my back. Something had happened there, something I couldn't explain and didn't like. Or I *did* like it—too much, and that was the problem.

This man admitted a mere hour ago to killing dozens of people in the Great Freeze, and then threatened to break off his healer's hand. I wasn't going to let a little snow dazzle that out of my memory.

"Oh, well, alright, let's go inside." My mother laughed nervously as I stomped away and back towards the house.

I didn't want to like Lucien Thorne. This complicated things. I had heard too many horrible stories to just fall for his charms. But charming he was. Soon enough his true colors would show and then I would shine a light on them and force him to see that I could never love a man like him. At the very least, we would tolerate each other for the sake of the kingdom and any future children we had.

The mere thought of having children with him caused my cheeks to heat up.

"Darling!" my mother called after me, and I stopped and turned to face her. Piper had disappeared into the greenhouse, and my father and King Thorne were talking far off in the meadow.

She was smiling. "Well, how's it going? He seems very... likable."

"A superb actor no doubt," I told her, and glared across the meadow at him.

My mother frowned. "That dowry... it was double what your father planned to ask for. Would an *actor* be so generous?"

My heart beat frantically in my chest at her assessment. "I suppose not."

A coy smile pulled at her lips as she hooked her arm in mine. "I've invited over some of our favorite courtiers. We can dance, drink, and get to know him better. That way you feel more comfortable going off on tour with him tomorrow."

I didn't want a spectacle, but I knew if the elders had already been told, then the entire court knew, or they would soon enough. That's what the tour was all about. Let all of the town gossips come out to see us together and spread the news.

The winter king had chosen a wife.

"Should I change my dress?" I asked my mother.

She nodded. "Nothing wrong with that one, but it's best that the king know we have provided well for you thus far."

That was my mother, always thinking of how others might perceive her and my father. In her defense, it was practically in the job title.

I veered into my room and prepared to get to know this man I was about to marry. I prayed to the Maker that some ghastly flaws would soon show themselves, otherwise I might have to change my mind about him. And I wasn't prepared to do that just yet.

REDHEADS LOOKED best in emerald green and dark purple but there was another secret color that made men's necks crane to look at us in adoration. A secret color you wouldn't expect.

Red.

Because my hair was more of a copper shade, the blood red dress I wore now, along with my green eyes, made my hair color pop even more. It was a fashion forward dress that I'd had recently made for one of Maxwell's parties. The neckline was appropriate but just barely so, and it hugged my hips, tightly clinging all the way to the knee before it belled out. The train was small enough that I could walk the room but long enough to be dramatic. I absolutely loved it.

"If he doesn't marry you, I will," Piper stated as she took in my gown.

I grinned. "It is a lovely dress, isn't it?"

Piper was wearing a beautiful pale blue gown with her brown hair tied up in a cascade of curls. "It is. And was that a moment I noticed between you two when you were showing off your powers together?" She stepped up beside me and started to pin the sides of my hair back.

I rolled my eyes. "The powers thing was... cool, but there was no *moment*."

Piper raised one eyebrow to me. "I asked the staff. They all said that he's been lovely and he even apologized for spilling water and offered to clean it himself."

My mouth popped open and I turned to looked at her. I didn't even do that. I apologized of course but the servants cleaned it up. That was their job.

"What is he playing at?" I asked her.

She simply shrugged. "You'll have to get to know him better to find out."

My hair was fully down and curled but for the sides pinned back away from my face. Piper pulled a metal tube of lip rouge out of her pocket and grinned at me.

"Is that my mother's?" I inquired.

She nodded. "She caught me stealing it twenty minutes ago and then told me to give it to you."

I smacked her arm playfully. "Piper! I don't need to woo him, we are already engaged."

Red lipstick was for enticing a man. I'd already gotten him.

Piper puckered her lips, motioning that I do the

same. I did, and as she applied the rouge she looked me in the eyes. "Madelynn, my mother gave me some love advice when I got my first brassiere, and I'm going to share it with you."

I steeled myself. Piper's mother was the lady-in-waiting to my own mother. She singlehandedly helped my mother manage her *entire* life. If she had advice, I wanted it.

"What?" I murmured as she pulled the stick of rouge away from my lips and then spun me in front of the mirror so that I could see myself.

Holy fae.

I looked... like I wanted to lure a husband.

"The advice was, that even when you're married, you still need to woo your man," Piper said with a smile.

I chuckled. "She said that?"

She dipped her chin. "So whether you're engaged, or married, or celebrating fifty years together, you need to woo." She winked.

"I don't want to woo him!" I snapped, and then felt badly for it. "I'm sorry. I'm just... he killed those people in the Great Freeze, he admitted it. My gran—"

"Had a weak heart and shouldn't have been out in the cold. That was years ago and he said he lost control. It sounded like an accident. Is he not allowed to make mistakes?"

I didn't like that she was sticking up for him, but was that because I was being too hard on him?

"He threatened to break off his own healer's hand!" I told her.

Piper nodded. "He's king and the healer was going against his wishes that you not be checked, which you should be grateful for!"

Piper was always so levelheaded. I hated it sometimes.

"Fine, let's just go to dinner." I smoothed my dress, trying not to be flustered. I expected Lucien Thorne to waltz in here and be a jerk. To lowball my dowry and beat our servants. I didn't know what to do with *this* man who had showed up.

MY MOTHER SAID a few favorite courtiers but what she meant was the elders, their spouses, over two dozen courtiers, and their families. The ballroom was filled to the brim with our entire house staff running around filling drinks or setting out food.

"Mother, this is grander than the Fall Festival," I said under my breath as I walked up to her. She took in my red lip rouge, my dress, and my heeled shoes.

"Madelynn, you have grown into a truly stunning

woman." Her eyes misted over with tears and it caught me off guard.

"Thank you," I said. "But this dinner party is too much."

My mother reached up and grasped my chin, shaking it a little. "It's not every day my eldest daughter gets betrothed. Let me have a little fun."

I sighed, relenting a little. My mother loved parties, loved decorating and going over the menu with the head chef. This was probably in the works for days.

I raised an eyebrow at her. "How long have you been planning this?"

She pursed her lips. "The winter king made his intentions known a few weeks ago but I had no idea what your father would decide."

"A few weeks!" I whispered-screamed. They kept this from me for a *few weeks*?

When people looked over at us, my mother gave a nervous laugh and raised her wine glass, then she glanced at me. "There were many back and forth exchanges. Your father made sure King Thorne and you would be a good match."

There was no sense arguing about something that was already done. "Lovely party, Mother. Thank you," I said dryly, and went in search of Piper.

She would share my disdain for a giant betrothal dinner I had no say in. I weaved in and out of the packed gathering of people, giving friendly smiles and thank yous when they offered congratulations. I was just turning away from Madame Fuller, my mother's and my favorite dressmaker, when I was suddenly standing before Lucien Thorne.

My breath hitched when I saw him in the silver silk tunic with snowflake embroidery at the hem. His eyes went half lidded as he assessed my dress and then settled on my red lips.

"I now know what it means when a man says a woman is breathtaking." He inhaled as if he'd truly forgotten how to breathe.

Another earth-shattering compliment I didn't know what to do with. The truth was, I was having trouble remembering how to breathe seeing him all dressed up.

Music started up in that moment and King Thorne wordlessly offered his hand to me. My mind screamed *no*, but my body leaned into his outstretched hand, and before I had a second to think about it, we were dancing. The room erupted into applause and the guests cleared the floor as the king expertly spun me around the dancefloor in my favorite waltz.

"You're a decent dancer," I commented, trying to get my wits about me. Being close to him like this, feeling his gentle hand on my lower back, my small hand tucked into his as I gripped his tight muscled arm with my free hand, it befuddled my common sense.

"Just decent? Oh, my mother would hate to hear that," he said with a frown.

I smiled. "Okay, more than decent. Did your mother teach you how to dance, King Thorne?"

"Please, call me Lucien," he said. "And yes, she did."

First name basis was usually done after the wedding, and even then the husbands insisted on my lord or Your Highness, even from a wife and queen. I heard a rumor that even his own father wasn't allowed to call him Lucien.

"Lucien, are you enjoying Fall Court?" I opted for small talk, as my mind and body were currently at war with each other. One part of me wanted to run away and the other wanted to know what he tasted like. It was horrifying and unexpected and I didn't know what to do.

He looked down at me, truly looked at me, with a depth I was sure climbed into the place where I kept my darkest secrets.

I felt raw and exposed under that gaze, and yet I couldn't look away.

"What is there not to like?" he asked. "Your countryside is stunning, your family and courtiers are very kind, and you are... beyond what I ever imagined."

Now it was my turn to lose my breath. The things he said, the constant compliments, it was... I didn't expect it. "Do you talk like this to all the women you want to woo?" I blurted out.

He laughed and his entire face lit up, the deep sound resonating within me. "Madelynn, you are the first woman I have wooed in quite some time. I just speak from the heart, as my mother taught me to."

I didn't know what to say to that, so I merely blinked rapidly and danced the rest of the song in silence. I felt a small stab of jealousy that he had wooed someone else a long time ago, and then felt stupid for it. I was overjoyed when dinner was announced and we all took our seats. Piper was seated on my left, and Lucien on my right, at the head of the table where my father usually sat. This time, my mother and father sat across from us.

Libby was sleeping and hated to miss parties, so I'd be sure to save her a piece of chocolate cake.

Our head servant, Jericho, approached the king with a deep bow. "Would you prefer red or white wine, Your Royal Highness? Or perhaps some local mead. We have an apple pumpkin ale that is famous with the locals."

Lucien held up a hand. "None, thank you. I don't drink."

I stiffened a little, sharing a look with my mother.

Men who didn't drink did so for only one reason: they had a problem with it.

It all made sense now. The stories of his outbursts, freezing the realm, cutting out a courtier's tongue. All things an unhinged man would do while drunk.

Jericho was a seasoned servant and knew protocol. If an honored guest refused drink, then no more wine was served to anyone at the party.

Instead of topping off my mother's empty glass or asking guests for their order, the wine and mead bottles slowly and silently left the room on the trays of our staff.

"My king, I do hope you love the meal. We are quite fond of our chef, and the meat was killed only hours ago in preparation." My mother was an expert at changing topics and defusing tension.

Lucien smiled at her kindly. "I cannot wait."

The rest of the night went smoothly. Lucien complimented the meal three times, going into detail about the rosemary-soaked stew and the sweet glaze on the potatoes. He was a polite guest and everyone seemed to be having a lovely time.

I, however, was abnormally quiet, envisioning a drunken king who'd turned to the bottle after the death of his mother. How long had he been sober? We had a problem in our court with one of the elders. He had a sickness, drank wine more than he did water. My mother had him sent away to an elvin healing center for this type of thing. He'd been sober ten years now.

I knew there had to be a flaw, a reason for the stories that surrounded him. We all had a past, and I wouldn't hold his against him so long as he was healed from it. That was the part that was bugging me.

Was he healed? I couldn't ask, it was not my place.

After dinner, the party broke up earlier than it usually did, probably from the lack of wine flowing, and I wished everyone a good night.

Tomorrow, we would start our multi-day tour of the courts. It would be the only time I would have to get to know the winter king before we were married forever.

As I stepped into the hallway with Lucien, I prepared to go right to my room as he would go left to the guest quarters, but instead he just stopped and looked down at me.

I paused, sensing he wanted to say something.

Reaching into his pocket, he pulled out an unknown object and kept it in his fist.

"I... was hoping you would wear this, but if you want to design your own I completely understand." He reached for my hand and dropped a delicate ring into it.

Looking down at the golden band with a snowflake design in the middle, I gasped.

"It was my mother's," he confessed, and my heart dropped into my stomach. "I know she would want you to have it."

Giving the bride a ring was customary after the dowry, but his mother's? It was very touching. I didn't know what to say.

"It's beautiful," I told him, and then slipped it onto my marriage finger. Seeing this ring on my hand made everything so real in that moment.

"Sleep well, Madelynn." He bowed lightly to me, which was unheard of, and again befuddled my mind.

"Goodnight, Lucien." I bowed lightly to him as we prepared to go separate ways to our rooms.

The way he said my name, delicately and with such care, it stayed on my mind long after I slipped into bed.

3

Libby did not take the news well. She cried and screamed and hugged me, and then ran to her room, locking herself in. My heart broke at her tantrum but I knew I'd be back in less than a week to see her again, so we set off on our tour of the four courts of Thorngate. Fall was first, and my people were thrilled for me, chanting my name and throwing flower petals at the carriage as we passed. But some of them glared at the king like he was a monster, like I had yesterday when I'd first met him.

I was at odds with the stories I'd heard and the man

before me. As we passed the last outlying fields of Fall, Lucien sat back into his seat of the carriage and looked out the open window. We would head to Spring now, and then Summer, and then his realm. *Winter*. After that, he would drop me back home and I wouldn't see him again until our wedding night. The entire trip would take about five days, and I had Piper at my side to stave off any rumors of impurity before the wedding night.

My parents would stay back in Fall with Libby and await my return.

I glanced at Piper, who was currently reading a steamy romance book I'd loaned her, then my gaze flicked to the king's movements. He carried no weapon, which was common with the highly powerful fae in our realm, and he was very clean. If one speck of lint marred his pants, he would pull it off and flick it out the open carriage window.

"King Th—" I started, and then remembered he'd asked me to call him by his first name. "Lucien, tell me about yourself. What do you do for fun? What makes you happy?" If I was going to be chained to this man for the rest of my life, I might as well get to know him better.

He bristled at the simple question, his gaze going from Piper to me, and then staring out the window at the passing trees.

An awkward silence stretched through the carriage and I wondered if he was going to ignore the question when he finally spoke.

"Honestly, I can't remember the last time I was truly happy. Sometime before my mother died probably. I used to like riding horses."

His honest answer reached into my chest and squeezed every last drop of blood from my heart. I felt Piper stiffen beside me but she stayed glued to her book. He didn't know what made him happy? His mother died when he was sixteen. He was twenty-one now... he hadn't felt happiness in five years? It was heartbreaking.

Had he given up horseback riding for fun after his mother's tragic accident? I swallowed hard, knowing there was something deeper there, but also knowing I could not go near it. Was that why he started drinking wine and then had a problem with it?

"Oh, well, I shall have to try and change that and find something to make you happy," I told him.

Yesterday I hated the man and now I was vowing to make him happy? *What is happening?*

His steely gray gaze met mine and my entire body melted under his look. His gaze traveled down my dress to my exposed ankles and he grinned. "I can think of some ways you could make me happy."

Piper sucked in a breath and I gasped, reaching out

to smack his shoulder playfully. "Lucien Thorne, you can't speak like that. It isn't appropriate." I glanced to Piper for backup but she was glued to her book. Fake glued to it, because she was totally hiding a smile.

Lucien leaned forward, giving me a devilish look. "I never was good at being appropriate."

Good night!

This man was... outrageous! I fell back into the seat, heat flushing my entire chest. I snuck glances at him, waiting for him to laugh and tell me he was kidding, but he never did.

He wasn't.

I decided then that it was safer to not speak at all. I wasn't sure how to handle Lucien Thorne. I liked it a lot better when I hated him and imagined him as a cruel, abusive prick. But this man wasn't that. He wasn't black or white, he was gray, and I didn't know what to do with gray.

BY THE TIME we reached Spring Court it was dark and we went straight to the Spring palace, where the duke and duchess were hosting us. The second I stepped out of the carriage, Princess Sheera squealed and ran for me. I laughed as she pulled me into a hug.

"Betrothed to the winter king! Come, we must talk." She pulled on my hand, but then stopped.

Lucien stepped out of the carriage with Piper then, and Sheera bowed deeply, as her parents stepped up behind her.

"Welcome to Spring Court, Your Highness." Sheera's voice was clipped and her glare evident. She didn't like him.

"Thank you." Lucien's voice was just as clipped.

As Lucien and the duke and duchess spoke, Sheera pulled me into the palace. I inhaled the warm night air as we went. I loved spring—not as much as fall of course but who could deny the beauty of the purple flowers that lined the walkway? Of the fragrant breeze that stayed in the air and smelled of an approaching rain.

I stared at Sheera's honey brown hair and dark brown skin, which were all in a stark contrast to her icy blue eyes. The tips of her pointed ears were painted with glitter dust, and I smiled at the latest fashion. Sheera always knew what the up-and-coming styles were.

I came twice a year to visit her on Spring Equinox and a leader's event my parents attended, and she did the same to me. Four times a year we got to stay up all night talking about boys, powers, who we would one day marry. Never in my wildest dreams did I think Lucien Thorne would be my betrothed.

Once we were in her room with the door closed, she spun. "Tell me everything. Is he awful? Has he hurt you?" she said in a rush. "We can run away together, hide out in Cinder Mountain if we need to."

I processed her questions rapidly, not blaming her for thinking Lucien was a monster, I had thought the same thing yesterday morning. And maybe he still was, but not to me. Not that I had seen.

"He's... kind of... sweet?" I wasn't even sure if my assessment was correct. I barely knew the man, but he had let me negotiate my own dowry and paid me whatever I asked. He'd complimented me at every turn and made it seem as if he actually desired to marry me for more than the politics involved.

Sheera's dark brown eyebrows knotted together in the center of her forehead. Reaching out, she touched my cheek. "Are you ill? You just called Lucien Thorne *sweet*."

A nervous peal of laughter escaped me and I began to pace the room.

"Madelynn, he froze the entire realm, killing dozens. And since then it's been story after story of his menacing rule. *Sweet* is not how I would describe him." Her voice was sharp and cutting. I'd never heard her like this.

"Well, he's been... accommodating," I amended. "My staff said he was nice to them as well."

She watched me pace her room. "Because he wants your power." She stepped in front of me and I stopped to face her. "Maddie, it's well known that you are the second-most powerful fae next to him. He will tell you anything to get you to marry him and have his heirs."

I frowned. Was that what he was doing? Being fake nice to me so that I wouldn't put up a fight?

"I told him I don't want children at first. He said that was okay."

Sheera laughed. "Don't be that naïve. The second you marry him the mask will drop and his true nature will show. You'll be pregnant within the first month and he'll be forcing you to fight at his side."

I frowned. "Fight? Fight who?"

She looked like she'd said too much, casting a glance over her shoulder at the door.

I placed a hand on my dearest friend's shoulder and forced her to look at me. "Sheera, fight who?"

She swallowed hard. "I overheard my parents saying that the winter king is pledging his army to join an upcoming battle with the elves and the dragon-folk."

My eyes grew wide. "A joint battle with Archmere and Embergate? Against who—?" But as soon as I said it I knew. "The Nightfall queen." She made life Hades for the other realms but she left us relatively alone thanks to Lucien. I'd heard that Lucien let the frost and snow from his border cross over into her land every once in a while to remind her what he was capable of. It must have worked, because she left us alone for the most part.

Sheera leaned into me. "Spring and Summer don't want war. We won't send soldiers to die for the winter king so that he can help his buddies."

I licked my lips. "Well, if he demands it, then you would have no choice."

She shrugged. "If he's not our king anymore, then he can't demand it."

Confusion pressed in on me. What was she saying? How could Lucien not be king anymore? Unless...

"Sheera, is your father going to try to overthrow King Thorne?"

Her face went stony still as if she were assessing me, no longer looking at me as a dear friend but more as the newly betrothed queen to who I was now realizing was her family's enemy.

"We should go to dinner. I don't want to keep my father waiting," she said, and then pulled me from the room.

My heart dropped into my stomach at her dismissal of my question. I knew that by being close to Winter's border, my father naturally aligned with King Thorne on most things, but did that mean that Spring and Summer were going to stage a coup? My mind spun with this information as we walked the halls of Spring Court to the large dining room. A few days ago I wouldn't have minded learning this new information, but today... I was torn.

When we entered the dining hall, the duke and duchess of Spring turned to greet us. Lucien sat at the head of the table, in the place of honor, and I noticed the seat beside him was empty, for me.

Piper was gone, which meant she'd either been asked to stay away or had chosen to do so. I didn't blame her. She and Sheera never really got along.

Sheera's mother, Petra, stood to kiss my cheek. "Madelynn, it's been too long since we've hosted you. What a surprise to find out about the upcoming nuptials."

Her careful wording was interesting. She called it a surprise but not a joyous one. Could I blame her? Our families were close and Lucien was hated across the fae realm. She was probably terrified for me.

"Thank you, Petra." I kissed her cheek back. We were long past the Mr. and Mrs. or Princess this and that. We'd been on a first name basis since I was ten.

"Well, what King Thorne wants, King Thorne gets," Sheera's father, Barrett, said.

Another dig.

"Yes, and don't you forget it." Lucien raised his water glass and sent a chilling glare at the duke.

This is not going well.

"I think we will make a good pairing, and the realm will benefit from our partnership," I said in the most diplomatic way possible. I barely knew the guy; I couldn't say that I loved him or was excited to marry him. It would be untrue, and obvious that I was trying to quell the rising discomfort in the room. Lucien locked eyes with me and nodded.

"I agree. Two of the most powerful fae ruling over the kingdom. What more could the people want?"

I knew he was partly marrying me for my power, but hearing him say it like that did make me think of what Sheera had just said in her room. She looked at me as if to emphasize her point. I swallowed the lump in my throat and took a seat next to the king.

"The people want continued peace, Your Highness," Duke Barrett said. "Rumors of war with the Nightfall queen have made their way to us, and I have to be bold and say that the people of Spring and Summer want nothing to do with that."

My entire body flinched at his boldness. I looked to Lucien, who set his glass down and glared at Barret. "You speak for Summer now too, Barrett?"

The room suddenly plunged twenty degrees as a chill formed in the air.

Barrett shifted in his seat. "Well, no, but we've communicated on this issue and we are in agreement."

Lucien nodded. "Well, *I'm* king, and if I think we need to go to war, you will mount your horse and ride at my side or I will have you imprisoned for treason."

Holy Maker, he just said that out loud. I was again witnessing his famous temper, but I hadn't expected it to be aimed at my dear friend's father. Still, he didn't raise his voice, or stab anyone in the chest with ice. No one's tongue was cut out. He was a king asserting his dominance over someone in his realm. Could I blame him? What Barrett said was cowardice. If we went to war, we would need all four courts' help.

"I thought this was supposed to be a celebratory dinner for our engagement. No more talk of war, okay?" I dropped my voice into the syrupy sweet range that I used when I wanted something from my father, and the men's glaring session broke as they both smiled tightly at me.

Petra raised her glass. "To the newly engaged couple. Long may you reign."

We all clinked glasses and then tucked into the most awkward dinner of my life. Silence, clanking forks, talk of the weather which was completely controlled by the men at the table, and more silence. After an hour, everyone feigned exhaustion and we all shut ourselves away into our rooms. By the time I got back to my sleeping quarters I was so glad to see Piper. She looked to have just finished unpacking my things in the bedroom. There was an adjoining guest room next door that she could sleep in.

"How was it?" she asked brightly as I entered.

"Pretty awful," I admitted as I kicked off my shoes and turned for her to unzip my dress.

"Oh no, what happened?" she inquired as she pulled the zipper down and I stepped out of my gown.

I told her about the conversation I'd had with Sheera in hushed tones as she drew me a bath. Sitting there in my undergarments, I then told her what the king had said when Barrett mentioned he didn't want war.

Piper shrugged. "Can you blame the king? He needs one hundred percent loyalty. If he calls for a war and there is dissent, lives will be lost on our side as the battle would be weak."

I smiled at Piper; she'd make a wonderfully brilliant royal advisor. Her mind worked in a way mine did not as she always had a good perspective of both sides.

"I cannot blame him and he did not lose his temper," I told her as I stripped down and sank into the bath.

Piper squeezed the liquid soap into the water to make bubbles and turned off the tap. Once the bath was drawn, she usually left me, but this time she knelt down and looked me in the eyes. "I cannot blame Duke Barrett either though. War is good for no one, and if the duke doesn't believe in the cause, then his men die in vain."

She left me with that and I felt unsettled for a long while after. What was she saying? Did I side with my soon-to-be husband and king, or did I side with one of my oldest friends, Sheera and her family?

4

The next day we passed through Spring Court and greeted the people, taking their well wishes with us. The well wishes were sparse. Only half the town came out to greet us, and most did so with a look of obligation. It was nothing like the Fall Court reception we'd had, and I imagined only slightly better than we would receive at Summer. The prince of Summer, Marcelle Haze, and the winter king had a longstanding feud. After Lucien froze over thirty of his people, the prince of Summer had stormed the Winter palace and demanded reparations and an apology. From what I'd heard, what he got was a beating.

The carriage left Spring lands as we ventured into Summer, and I looked over at Lucien. Who was this man? His history was so mysterious and dark and filled with fantastical stories.

"Are we going to war with the Nightfall queen?" I asked suddenly.

Piper was beside me knitting and pretended to be overly interested in the stitching pattern in that moment.

Lucien stared at me seriously, his eyes darkening. "I haven't decided."

His tone said it was the end of discussion, but I crossed my arms and glared at him. "Why would we?" I snipped. "Things are peaceful and she doesn't bother us!"

He leaned forward, edging into my space, and I swallowed hard. "Do you know why she doesn't bother us?"

He wanted an ego fluff, fine. "Because of you. She fears you."

He nodded. "She fears me *but* still hates our kind. She will pick off the dragon-folk and elves first, then the wolves. Then she will come for the fae last so by that time it will be too late for us to band together and overthrow her. But make no mistake, she will come for us one day. The question is, do we go for her first?"

Holy fae, his words sent goosebumps down my arms and I couldn't help the terror that climbed into my heart. The Nightfall queen hated magical persons yes, but... but she didn't bother us.

Why? Because Lucien was right?

I suspected he was, and I couldn't help but feel in that moment he was king for a reason.

He was clearly the best man for the job, cunning, powerful and slightly scary.

"Do I get a vote?" I asked. "When we marry, will you consult with me before you go throwing our people into war? Or will I just be some decorative queen that stands by your side and looks pretty?"

He looked pained at my accusation and I instantly regretted it. "Of course. I will cherish your council, but in the end I will do what it takes to protect you in the long run, even if you hate me for it."

He had this uncanny ability to say romantic things that were also kind of scary.

A smirk pulled at his lips and his eyes ran from the top of my head to my crossed ankles. "I also think you make a pretty ravishing decoration."

Piper snort-laughed beside me and then immediately swallowed the sound.

My cheeks heated and I wanted to open the

window and get some fresh air. "I don't know what to think about you," I confessed in frustration.

He laughed, and the entire air shifted. It was deep, throaty, and had a way of crawling under your skin and caressing your heart.

I love his laugh, I thought to myself guiltily.

"Are you disappointed I have not cut out anyone's tongue yet?" He grinned.

I gasped, and even Piper set down her knitting to look at the king.

"Well... yes, to be honest," I told him.

That laugh rang out through the carriage again and I felt like a fool.

"What's so funny? Surely not cutting out a man's tongue!" I snapped, reaching out to poke his chest.

His hand snaked out and caught mine, clasping my fingers lightly as a shock of ice cold zipped up my arm. His gray eyes bored into me then and it felt like he was seeing my very soul. The way he gazed at me was unlike any look a man had ever given me. It made my stomach drop and warm at the same time.

"I became king at sixteen, shortly after my mother died. My father abdicated in his prime, which made our family look weak. How else was I to ensure my position so that no one would come to dethrone me?"

Our fingers were still touching, and I couldn't get

that out of my mind enough to process his words, but Piper gasped next to me, clearly getting his reasoning.

"You made up the stories," Piper said.

Lucien smiled at Piper. "Yes. I paid my palace staff to spread rumors that I was a horrible, powerful, vengeful king."

Shock ripped through me, and I finally pulled my fingers from his. "You didn't! But... people hate you for those stories."

He shrugged, peering at me coolly. "I'd rather be a hated and feared king than a challenged and dead one."

My mind spun with this new revelation. He wasn't wrong. The way his father became king was to challenge and fight the previous king, killing him and taking his place. It was our way. But no one challenged a powerful king who was known to fly off the handle at any moment and cut out a tongue.

"That's... You..." I couldn't find the words.

"Genius?" Lucien offered, raising one eyebrow and looking impossibly handsome.

I scoffed. "Well, the rumors of your lack of humble nature are true I see."

Lucien just smirked as if he enjoyed ruffling my feathers. It all made sense now, why the man who had shown up to negotiate my dowry was a far cry from the ruthless menace I'd heard stories about.

"But the Freeze, that was real. I lived through it. You admitted as much," I told him, indicating the night so many across our realm died.

He sighed, his face falling as a haunted look took over him. "Yes, well, not everything is a rumor. I'm not a perfect man."

A deep sadness crept into my heart then. I didn't know why I thought all these years that he didn't carry any regret over that night, but the look on his face, like I'd shot his beloved pet, told me all I needed to know.

That night was a mistake, and he regretted everything about it.

I reached out and grasped his hand tenderly. "I have trouble controlling my powers too sometimes," I told him. It was a bit of a lie. I rarely lost control, and when I did, it was easy to rein back in.

He looked at me flatly. "Have you ever killed over fifty people with a windstorm that you created and couldn't stop?"

I dropped his hand and leaned back into the seat. This was clearly a touchy topic, and I didn't want to push him anymore.

"No," I admitted, and we settled into a silent ride. Everything he had said filled the air. My mind chewed over every single word.

He lied. The cut-out tongues, the dragging staff from horses as punishment... all of those insane stories of a cruel king... were lies. It was also kind of genius, like he'd said. No one dared challenge the ruthless winter king. The Thorne family ruled for generations, only having been dethroned a few times but always winning the kingship back with the next heir. It's why our realm was named Thorngate.

When Lucien's mother died, there were rumors that it broke his father and that's why he'd abdicated. Lucien had to step up and become king at sixteen years old or someone would have come for his father. They would have challenged him and killed him.

But the Freeze was real, and he did have a cold personality at times, so there was a story there but not enough to make him the monster I'd spent my entire life believing he was. The longer we drove, the more the guilt of what Sheera had told me was eating me up inside and I could no longer contain it. This was my future husband, the father of my future children, *my king*.

"Lucien, if I told you a secret, would you promise not to retaliate or punish the person in question?" I said as Piper went rigid beside me.

Lucien slowly looked up at me through steel gray eyes. "I can make no such promise, but I will do my best."

I chewed at my lip, knowing that now that I had

mentioned it I would have to say something, but also that I didn't want to indicate Sheera.

One gift the king had, that all the kings across Avalier had, was the power to detect a lie.

Careful with my wording, I cleared my throat. "Be careful with Duke Barrett. I heard a rumor he might like to overthrow you one day."

There, the truth, and it protected my friend.

Lucien relaxed. "That old man couldn't win a fight against me. No, if Barrett wants me dethroned, it will be Prince Haze who fights me. They will team up together, probably also talking your father into it and coming at me together somehow."

My mouth popped open at his bleak assessment. Prince Haze of Summer Court, who we were on our way to see right now, was the most powerful summer fae in a generation. He could light fires with his hands and send sunrays so bright into your face that they blinded you.

"You've thought about this," I noted.

Lucien looked coolly across the carriage at me. "I'm the most hated man in Thorngate. My enemies are many." His voice was monotone, but there was an underlying hurt there. Like he didn't want to be hated.

"My father wouldn't—" I began to defend him but Lucien held up a hand.

"I'm not accusing. I'm just saying it's a possibility,

especially if Prince Haze threatened to scorch all of his crops."

I crossed my arms. "Like you have threatened to freeze ours in the past?"

Lucien relaxed easily into the seat, raising his arms above his head and hooking his fingers behind his neck. "Yes, well, I know how to get what I want, don't I?"

I huffed. He was absolutely incorrigible! *And* insanely attractive. It was infuriating.

I felt at odds with the situation. Did I like the winter king or did he annoy me to no end? Maybe a little of both. And maybe that's what marriage was. Or at least what *this* marriage was about to be. Part of me wanted to slap Lucien Thorne across the face, and the other part wanted to kiss him.

THE SECOND we reached the Summer Court gates, I knew something was wrong. The gates were closed and a line of a dozen guards stood before them.

"What's going on? Aren't they expecting us?" I asked. We'd sent word to all the realm of our engagement the moment after we negotiated my dowry.

Lucien's jaw grit and his nostrils flared. The carriage pulled to a stop and he stepped out. I moved to follow him and he held up a hand. "Stay here. I will handle this."

I pushed his hand down. "I'm going."

He cast me an annoyed look but helped me out of the carriage. We walked together past the Winter Soldier on horseback and to the lead Sun Guard at the front of the gates.

"What do you think you are doing barring your king from entering a territory in *my* lands," Lucien spat. A gust of a cold wind stirred at our backs.

Okay, not the first thing I would have said to the guard, but I was learning that the rumors of Lucien's hot temper were *very* real. Just minus the tongue cutting out.

The lead guard stepped forward and pulled a scroll from his sleeveless vest. The Summer sun insignia on his breastplate glinted in the bright sunlight, and I tried to keep things calm.

"Greetings, I'm Madelynn Windstrong, the princess of Fall," I told the guard in case he didn't know who he was dealing with.

"I know who you are," he said flatly.

Lucien bristled at that. Suddenly a blade of ice shot out from his palm and pressed against the guard's throat. Every soldier present spurred into action then, pulling out their blade or conjuring sunlight in their palms.

74

"*You* are a lowly guard, so when you address a princess you will call her by her title," Lucien growled at him.

"Yes, my king," the guard mumbled, eyes wide.

Lucien pulled the ice blade from the man's throat and it clattered to the ground, breaking into a dozen pieces.

I was frozen in shock, unable to react by the time it was all over. The other guards didn't seem to know what to do. Were they really going to attack their king? Their allegiance was to the prince of their court, but above all was the king of our fae realm and *that* was Lucien.

They seemed to remember this in that moment, and one by one put away their blades and defused their sunlight powers.

Lucien glared at them each in turn.

"Tell me what the Hades is going on right now or I'll turn you all into icicles!" he shouted.

The scroll was still clenched in the guard's hand, and he gave it to me with trembling fingers.

I tugged on it, pulling it open.

When I read the first few lines, my stomach dropped.

"They want to divide the realm," I mumbled.

Lucien turned to me, looking over the document. It said that the Summer prince, Marcelle Haze, was petitioning the realm for separation. He wanted to be king of his own realm, which would include Spring Court, and he proposed the name Hazeville.

Every second Lucien read, the temperature dropped. Snow began to fall from the sky and clouds blotted out the sun.

Oh no.

"He can't do this," Lucien growled.

So this was what Sheera had been talking about.

The lead guard looked terrified. He cleared his throat and stared at the king. "He can, Your Highness. Bylaw states that the entire realm has to vote, and if at least two of the four courts are in agreement, it passes."

Summer and Spring.

No.

The coldness seeped into my skin then and my teeth started to chatter.

I quickly hooked my arm with Lucien and pulled him aside. I grasped the sides of his face and forced him to look into my eyes. "Calm down. This isn't the way to handle it." My hot breath puffed out into white fog before me. I'd heard of the winter king's power but until I looked into his eyes and could have sworn I saw snow falling in his irises, I wasn't sure just how connected to the elements he was. In that moment it was as if he was made of winter: stone cold skin, snowy eyes—even his lips looked coated in frost.

Lucien held my gaze. "If they want to separate, then they will become my enemy. I will bring war to their gates, kill Prince Haze, and take them back!" he roared.

I understood his anger. Half of his kingdom had just declared treason. The betrayal would sting, especially after he'd protected them for the past six years. The snow was dumping now, falling in huge clumps that landed on everything, including my eyelashes.

I blinked them away and focused on the storm before me, the storm brewing in Lucien's eyes. "Everyone here hates you," I told him honestly. "You killed over thirty of their people and never apologized. If you want them to hate you more, then sure, send another storm their way, but I think we should go home, get married, and prove that you are stronger than ever with a powerful and loyal queen at your side."

At my words, his eyes cleared, the clouds parted, and the snow stopped. The sunlight came back out, the heat melting off the snow and turning it into water that ran into the gutters beside the road. I was amazed at how quickly he was able to turn things around.

My chest was heaving. I had been two seconds away from using my wind magic to push his snow back, but I was glad I'd not done that. It was clear to me now that Lucien didn't trust many people and I didn't want him to put me on the list of ones he couldn't count on.

I pulled my hands from his face and Lucien adjusted his tunic, reaching up to smooth his damp hair. "No, we will go in and show the people of Summer that they have a strong king and soon-to-be-queen right now. No need to separate." Then he simply walked back over to the guard and looked him in the eyes.

"I recognize your request for separation and will hold a realm-wide vote when I get back to Winter Court," Lucien said calmly. "Until then, it is your duty to host your king and future queen. Failure to do so will be a declaration of war."

Future queen.

I knew that was to be my title, but hearing him say it made warmth spread throughout my limbs. It was a powerful position, one I'd never imagined holding.

The guards all looked at each other in confusion, and finally the lead guard nodded and leaned into a messenger. "Bring word to Prince Haze that the winter king and Princess Windstrong are on their way."

The messenger got on his horse and the gates opened. He disappeared behind them, taking off at a gallop.

The guard then indicated we get back in our carriage, and so Lucien and I walked over to it. When we reached the door, Lucien looked to me, bending down close to my ear. "If Prince Haze tests my patience, I will not hesitate to challenge him right here and now."

I swallowed hard, my eyes widening. "Is now a bad time to mention he was my first kiss?"

The color drained from Lucien's face, his mouth popping open in shock before uncontrolled anger crossed his face and every single muscle tightened, snapping his jaw shut.

I burst into laughter. I couldn't help it, he was so easy to upset. Doubling over with giggles, I had to grasp his forearms to keep upright. When I finally stood, there were tears leaking from my eyes.

"You were *so* jealous," I managed to get out between fits of laughter.

He looked amused. "I can't wait to pay you back for that one."

My face went slack. "What? Hey, I was joking. I've never touched him."

Lucien shrugged. "Watch your back, Windstrong," he taunted, and then spun, slipping into the carriage.

"Retaliation for a simple joke is *not* very gentlemanly," I reminded him as I popped into the carriage and took a seat next to Piper.

He gazed back at me with a devastatingly handsome glare. "I never claimed to be a gentleman."

Oh Hades, what have I gotten myself into?

As our carriage pulled through the Summer Court gates, the king and I peered out the window and waved as we passed by. People looked surprised to see us, which meant that Prince Haze hadn't told them of our arrival and never expected us to actually come inside.

My memories of Marcelle were few and far between but he wasn't a stupid man. Did he really think the winter king would just leave without a fuss?

No. He'd expected Lucien to bring a storm of snow and probably drench the town in coldness, further adding votes to his cause.

"Marcelle wanted you to lose your temper," I said.

"Yes," Lucien agreed. "And I would have gladly given him the storm he desired had you not stopped me."

"Covering Summer Court in frost would have added votes to the separation," I added, and Lucien sat quietly with that. Sticking my head out the window, I waved to some small children.

A little girl with flowers ran alongside the carriage and looked up at me. "It's Princess Madelynn! Make the wind come!" she yelled.

Children often begged royalty for displays of power, and this time I decided to oblige her. Pulling on a fraction of my power, I called the wind past her, causing her little blond curls to fly about her face. She squealed in delight and suddenly there was a coldness in the air as snowflakes fell into my wind, causing a mild flurry.

The little girl laughed even louder, throwing her arms into the air as the snow whipped around her. "It's snowing!" she squealed to the shop owners as they came out of their stores to see what the fuss was about.

I glanced at Lucien to find that he was watching me. I wasn't sure exactly how to interpret his gaze, but it looked a lot like how my father gazed at my mother when she did something especially adorable. As a royal of Fall Court, I had very little contact with men, so I wasn't sure how to read Lucien's advances. In my school days, I had managed to sneak behind the library a few times and kiss Dayne Hall, my boyfriend at the time, but I was a young teenager then. Now I was a woman... and this felt different.

One by one, the shop owners began to glare at the passing carriage, and I stopped my wind power. Lucien did the same, ceasing the light snow he had conjured.

"The little girl liked it," I told him, trying to find the lightness in the situation.

Lucien nodded.

The shops gave way to empty fields, and then we came upon a cemetery. I'd been to Summer Court as a little girl and then again at Midsummer Festival when I was thirteen, right before the Great Freeze. I didn't remember the cemetery being here but—

I sucked in a breath when I read the sign.

Lost to the Ice But Never Forgotten. Next to it was the year of the Freeze. The one Lucien caused to encompass the entire realm.

I looked at Lucien, praying he didn't see it, but he was staring at the small granite stones with such a profound sadness I wanted to cry. His chest silently heaved as his eyes darted around the graveyard and his face went slack.

He's counting them, I thought. *Counting the people he killed.*

"Stay here," Lucien barked, his voice cracking. Then he leapt out of the moving carriage. It screeched to a halt, kicking up dust as Piper and I shared a concerned look.

"What's he doing?" Piper asked.

I shrugged, leaning forward to peer out the curtain. As the dust settled, I saw Lucien's tall form passing by the gravestones. As he approached each one, he pulled out his hand and touched the top of the stone, mumbling something under his breath.

"Is he making peace?" Piper murmured.

A tear lined my eye and I nodded. "I think so."

When he reached the last stone, he knelt because it was a small one. A child—no, a baby. When he touched this stone, an icicle formed in his palm and took the shape of a rose, which he laid at the base of the rock slab.

I couldn't watch any longer but I also couldn't look away. It was gut wrenching. I felt sick. I could practically feel his grief. The wind picked up, rushing past the carriage and slamming into Lucien as I fought to control my anguish. He clearly regretted his actions. And I'd clearly misjudged this king.

Lucien turned to look at the carriage and I wiped away the stray tear that had fallen onto my cheek and dropped my power over the wind, taking in a deep calming breath.

A few moments later, he stepped back inside and sat before me. Pulling the curtain shut, he didn't utter a single word. He just closed his eyes, like he wanted to shut the world away and just be lost in darkness and silence.

I glanced at Piper, unsure what to do, but she sat glued to her knitting, head down and pretending to be a fly on the wall like any decent chaperone would.

I didn't know Lucien that well yet. Did he want silence? Should I try to grasp his hand in comfort?

If only he would explain to everyone why he lost control of his powers and caused the Freeze all those years ago... it would help people to understand, for *me* to understand. But I knew now was *not* the time to bring that up.

"Why did the slice of bread get sent home from school?" I asked, and the king's eyes popped open, searching for me like a drowning man looked for a floatation ring. I needed to pull him out of this mood before he met the Summer prince, and if there was one thing I was good at, it was stupid jokes. I'd learned hundreds of them from my father. We spent hours in front of the fireplace thinking them up as a family.

"Bread doesn't go to school," Lucien said flatly, but there was some relief in his voice.

I rolled my eyes. "Play along. It's a joke. *Why* did the slice of bread get sent home from school?"

Lucien smirked. "He got in a fight with butter?"

I burst out into laughter, not expecting that reply, and my laugh made the corners of Lucien's mouth turn up. "No. He was feeling *crumby*."

Lucien shook his head. "That was really bad."

I nodded. "I have hundreds. Want to hear more?"

"Maker no. Please, never again," he said, but he was smiling.

"What do you call a potato with spectacles?" I asked.

Lucien covered his ears. "Make it stop."

I leaned forward, pulling one of his hands from his head. "A spec-tater."

Lucien groaned at the joke, but then we both realized at the same time that we were in super close proximity. I swallowed hard as I put a hand on his chest to push myself backwards and was met with rock hard muscle.

He caught my wrist as I tried to leave and looked me right in the eyes. "You're good for me, Madelynn Windstrong."

My breath hitched at the romantic sentiment and then the cart jerked to a stop.

I fell back into the seat, his hand yanking from mine.

You're good for me.

It was so sweet and also so *sad*, like he hadn't had a good person in his life in a long time.

The curtain pulled back suddenly and there was a lady's maid standing before us. She wore the yellow and orange uniform of Summer and curtsied deeply to me. "Greetings, Princess Madelynn. Prince Haze has given you the west wing guest quarters inside the palace for your stay."

I smiled and nodded to her as Piper started to gather our things.

The maid then looked at Lucien. "King Thorne..." She forced a tight smile. "Prince Haze has allocated his guest house, off palace property for you. You may join us for dinner."

"Oh may I?" Lucien growled, but I reached out and stroked the top of his hand. Off palace property was a slap in the face, but if Prince Haze was planning on separating the courts it was best not to make a fuss before the vote. Maybe a nice dinner would smooth things over.

"Lucien, darling..." I looked to my betrothed. "... why don't you get settled in and I'll see you for dinner."

His eyes went half lidded. "Alright, but only because you called me darling."

That caused me to smile. I couldn't help the flush of my cheeks as my face grew hot. This man was a charmer, and so far he only used these powers on me and not any of the other women in the vicinity, so I had to admit I quite liked it.

"Thank you," I whispered, and then stepped out of the carriage. When Piper disembarked, the carriage pulled away, taking Lucien away from the palace and to a small guest house in the distance, beyond the maze of beautiful gardens.

Piper helped the servants gather my bags just as I was staring out onto the rich gold and yellow flower garden.

"Princess Madelynn," a familiar but deeper-than-I-remembered voice called behind me. I turned to see Marcelle Haze, prince and lead royal of the Summer Court. He looked handsome in a gold silk tunic. His blond hair was cropped short, showing the tips of his pointed ears. "I haven't seen you since you were... thirteen?" His eyes roamed slowly over my entire body. "You... grew up." His voice dropped an octave and nervousness flushed through me. If Lucien had been here for that introduction, it would be snowing right now.

"I did. And I got engaged." I held up my hand, reminding him of his place.

He pursed his lips and stepped forward to inspect the ring Lucien had given me. "I didn't know you were open to suitors or I would have thrown my offer at your father as well."

"Marcelle," I warned, my tone cutting.

Every year or so from age six to thirteen, my family would come here with Sheera and her parents for Summer Solstice. Marcelle and his little brother Mateo would play with Sheera and I the entire week we were here. But his father became somewhat of an extremist, saying that Fall and Summer shouldn't be mixing, and stopped inviting us. It was clear that in his father's mind, Summer and Spring were one unit and Fall and Winter were another.

"Besides, your father would roll over in his grave if you married anyone from Fall Court," I teased.

Marcelle grinned. "True, but you would be worth it."

"Stop," I snapped, more harshly this time, and he held up his hands in defense.

"I'm glad to see you. No matter the circumstances." He glared in the distance at Lucien's retreating carriage and I frowned.

"Suggesting separation from Thorngate, Marcelle? Come on. That's not right. Surely there can be another arrangement to please you." I was going to take advantage of this friendly banter while I could.

Marcelle's eyes cut to mine. "I must go after what is best for my people, and yes that means separation from Winter and the madman that rules it."

"Your people are fae, same as mine, same as Lucien's. We're all one. There is no need to separate—"

"I do not want war with the Nightfall queen!" Marcelle snapped. "I have it on good authority that your betrothed would bring us in a realm-wide war with her. He's unhinged, as we all know."

I ignored his *unhinged* comment and thought about what Lucien had said. "You're right. He might. And if you separate, you won't have his protection. The Nightfall queen will come for you last, when you're weak and *alone*. Good luck with that, Marcelle."

I looked to Piper: "I'm tired. I'd like to lie down before dinner."

"Yes, my lady." Piper curtsied to me, ever the professional in front of other royals.

I stomped past Marcelle, reining in my emotions so that I didn't rustle the slightest breeze. I didn't want him to know how much our conversation bothered me.

Separation from the realm was unheard of! It made our people look weak and divided. All so that Marcelle could push off an eventual war with the Nightfall queen? It was cowardice.

ONCE SETTLED INTO OUR ROOMS, Piper came to sit at the edge of my bed as I angrily brushed out my hair.

"Dividing the fae realm will surely attract the Nightfall queen's notice," Piper said.

I growled in frustration. "I know."

She took the brush from my hand. "You're going to rip all of your hair out," she teased, and then started to brush my hair more gently.

I chuckled but couldn't bring myself to smile. "Everything rides on this dinner with Lucien and Marcelle, doesn't it?" I asked my closest ally.

She nodded. "If you can show Marcelle that Lucien is a reasonable man, maybe he will think twice about the separation."

The thing was, I wasn't sure Lucien *was* a reasonable man. Reasonable maybe, but also unpredictable and moody.

"He locked the winter king out of his own land. That's treason right there," I told Piper.

She nodded, setting the brush down and walking over to face me. Piper barely had any Fall Court powers; she couldn't rustle the wind and she wasn't good at gardening. But what she offered in advice and friendship far outweighed her lack of magic. I always cherished her advice, and I knew by the look on her face now that a heavy dose of it was coming.

"If you weren't here I suspect his snowstorm would have ravaged the town. The king is right, you are good for him," she said.

I blushed, but was also disturbed that she felt Lucien would have lashed out so easily.

Piper sighed. "I've watched the king carefully this entire trip, Madelynn. One thing is clear: he feels a deep remorse for the Great Freeze. It seemed to be an accident, one he doesn't know how to apologize for."

I nodded. "I agree, but the other courts don't see that. They only see his actions, and his lack of apology has allowed hatred for him to fester here for years."

Piper gave me a small smile, waiting for me to come around to what she was getting at. Her advice was always subtle, almost as if she wanted me to get the idea myself.

"You think I should ask Lucien to apologize to Marcelle tonight for the Great Freeze?" I said in shock.

Piper's grin grew wider. "I do."

The thought of asking a powerful king for such a humble act made me want to vomit. Lucien was a grown man, I was not yet his wife. Asking him to become vulnerable in front of an adversary like Marcelle was a big request. But Piper was right. It could pave the way to keeping the fae kingdom together.

"What if Marcelle doesn't take the apology well? What if he ridicules Lucien?"

Piper lifted her chin high. "Then you stand up for your king and your future husband and show him what having a powerful woman by his side will be like."

"Sounds like something Elowyn would do," I told her, remarking about one of our favorite romance novels by L. Ashta. She was a Winter fae who wrote under a pen name. Some of her novels were so steamy it wouldn't be appropriate to divulge her identity, but her heroines always stood up for their men and bedded them after.

"You like him," I told Piper. She was a very good judge of character, always telling me who to watch out for.

Piper smirked. "I do. I think he's misunderstood. He treats you well—in his own way—and I can see already that he adores you."

Adores me. That made my stomach flip over, and Piper pointed to my face. "This is the tenth time you've blushed today!" she accused.

I fell backwards on the bed laughing as she fell beside me.

Heaving a large sigh, I looked over at my best friend. "I've never had a man... say these things to me. Pursue me so... *aggressively.*"

Piper popped up on one elbow and looked down at me with a grin. "You like it?"

I tried to hide the smile but it came out anyway, causing us both to fall into fits of laughter.

"Maybe marrying Lucien won't be the worst thing on the planet," I told her.

Piper nodded. "Maybe it will be the best thing that ever happened to you. Like Elowyn and Rush."

Maybe it would. That thought kept the smile on my face for hours.

6

"I'm going to vomit," I told Piper as she pushed me towards the front door of Lucien's guest cottage. We'd walked here, enjoying the warm weather and sunshine, but the sun was beginning to set and we'd be expected at dinner soon. I needed to ask Lucien to apologize publicly to Marcelle for the Great Freeze and I felt sick about it. He was king, and asking a king to do anything was... bad mannered.

"You're his betrothed and future queen. You want what is best for him and the realm," Piper reminded me.

I nodded, letting out a shaky breath, and smoothed my palms over my emerald green dress. The neckline was definitely a little more scandalous than appropriate, but dressing stuffy like my mother never suited me, and Lucien didn't seem to mind.

Reaching up, I knocked at the door.

A moment ticked by, then another. I looked at Piper, wondering what was taking so long, when the door opened.

An audible gasp left my throat when I gazed upon Lucien's bare chest. Beads of water ran down his neck, rolling over each defined ab muscle before hitting the band of his trousers.

His hair was wet and he was drying it with a towel as his eyes raked over my dress. It was as if I could physically feel his gaze caressing me and it sent a warm zap of energy down my back. Averting my eyes, I held up a hand. "I'm so sorry," I said.

Lucien chuckled deeply. "If you're this shy with me tunicless, how will you feel when we finally make children?"

"Lucien!" I scolded him, turning to face him with an angry snarl.

But he was grinning, and I hated that he was enjoying ruffling my feathers.

"I need to speak with you. Can you please put some clothes on?" I asked him.

"You look beautiful. Let's skip dinner with Prince Haze and have dinner here together, just you and I," he said suddenly.

I swallowed hard, wanting to look at Piper for advice, but she'd scurried away and was now standing too far away in the courtyard, unable to hear us.

"Tunic please," I said again.

Maker, please put on a tunic before I beg Piper to leave so I can go inside alone.

He left the door open and stepped inside. I was surprised to see that there was no palace staff. His servants were gone and it seemed to just be him. When he came back out, he wore a black and silver silk tunic that matched his eyes.

"You look handsome," I told him shyly, figuring I would return his earlier compliment.

He smiled, his eyes smoldering as he looked at me. "Does that mean we will be bedding for more than just making children?"

"Lucien Thorne!" I reached out and smacked his chest, aghast at his inappropriate humor.

He caught my hand and pulled it to his lips, kissing the top. "I'm sorry, you're an easy target, sugar plum."

I scoffed at the pet name and tried to remember why I was here. He was still holding my hand; the spot he had kissed was tingling, sending waves of warmth into my gut. I couldn't tell if I hated his vulgar humor or liked it.

"You're blushing," he said.

"I'm warm!" I snapped, and pulled my hand back. "Let's take a walk." I moved outside into the courtyard. Piper moved as well, finding a small bench near the rose bushes to sit down on but still have view of us. Lucien stepped into the open air and squinted at the sun. It cast shadows on his pale skin, and a little bead of sweat formed on his upper lip.

I giggled. "You can't wait to get back to Winter Court, can you?"

He looked over at me. "Far too much sunshine for my liking. Would it kill him to pull some clouds over it for our visit?"

"The lack of a breeze is killing me! Who wants stagnant warm air?" I joined in his complaint and pulled at my dress to indicate how stifling I was.

Lucien stopped in front of me and looked down. We'd barely had time to be together as just us, and I realized now how tall he was. Most fae were tall—I certainly was—but Lucien was a head taller than me and I had to crane my neck to stare up at him.

"What do you want?" Lucien asked pointedly.

I shook myself, mouth popping open in shock. "Excuse me?"

Lucien smiled. "You did not drop by before dinner

dressed as dessert so that we could arrive together. You want something. Just tell me what it is so that I can give it to you."

Dressed as dessert. I wasn't even going to reprimand that comment, it was far too clever and I was starting to think Lucien wouldn't stop either way. Truth be told, I was starting to like the way he spoke to me. It was flattering, and made me feel beautiful and wanted.

"I had a little chat about the separation with Prince Haze upon my arrival," I started.

Lucien's face instantly went rigid. "Were you able to talk any sense into the buffoon?"

I blew air out through my teeth. "I tried. I told him that if he separated and we fought the queen, she would pick him off last and he wouldn't have your protection."

Lucien looked impressed by that answer. It was after all a play on his own answer to me.

Reaching out, I grasped his forearm. "But, Lucien, he doesn't see you as a reasonable man. All Summer Court sees are the graves they walk by each day and the lingering silence from you on what happened during the Great Freeze."

Lucien yanked his hand away from mine as if I'd burned him, and then he turned, giving me his back. The temperature plummeted suddenly, and although I was grateful for the reprieve in heat, I knew it was because he was upset. I walked around him and got right up in his face, forcing him to look at me.

"You never even said sorry. You didn't send a letter, just a bag of gold, which was an insult with no note to accompany it." My voice cracked as I thought of the night my grandmother died. "You are our king, our *protector*, and in one night you took people from us without a word of why."

The strangled sound of pure grief that ripped from his throat constricted my heart. He staggered backwards, clutching his chest as if I'd stabbed him. I couldn't believe that this entire time I thought him to be a cold monster who didn't care for anyone. Simply hearing my words had affected him so deeply and I regretted how hard I'd been with his pain. Rushing forward, I grasped his hands, pulling them to my stomach.

"I'm sorry. I was merely trying to get you to see how the others view you. How the silence has fed their hatred of you and therefore their desire to separate." I felt ashamed for causing this much emotion in him right before a big dinner with the prince of Summer. Had I known how deeply it would affect him, I never would have brought it up.

Lucien blinked rapidly and then cleared his throat. "I wrote a realm-wide letter a thousand times," he said, "but no words could do justice in explaining my actions. No words would give peace to those who had lost someone at my hand. No one wants excuses, they want their family member back."

"So you sent gold instead?" I asked him. The next day each court had gotten a little sack of gold for "damages." It looked callous. *Sorry for the death and destruction, here is some coin.*

He sighed. "I was young, without a mother for guidance. I didn't know how to handle it."

Reaching up, I tilted his chin down with my fingers to force him to look at me. "You're older now, Lucien. I think it's time for an apology—and an explanation of what happened that night."

He bristled, staring into my eyes with an unknown depth. There was so much pain there, and yet I saw anger too, like roiling clouds in a thunderstorm. What had happened that night? It was a few months after his mother's death, so I knew it couldn't have been solely that.

"I cannot explain, but if you think it will help I can apologize," he said, and then his eyes dropped to my lips.

"I think it would help." My fingers were still on his chiseled jaw, and I licked my lips, my chest heaving as I imagined what it would be like to kiss him.

Kissing a classmate behind school was one thing,

but kissing a king in a courtship was another. It wasn't done—not that I thought Lucien would mind breaking a modesty rule. Surely not in full view of the Summer courtiers! Protocol stated we would have our first kiss at the altar, before the Maker and our people.

Pulling my hand away from him, I stepped back and released a breath. Lucien cocked a smile and I glared at him. "What's so funny?"

Lucien leaned forward, whispering into my ear. "Watching you wrestle with how much you want me brings me great satisfaction."

Heat flushed through my entire body at that. I scoffed, "You think too highly of yourself." But I felt caught. I felt like maybe I wasn't hiding my thoughts as well as I hoped.

Lucien reached out and pulled a stray chunk of red hair behind my ear. "No, my sugar plum. I think too highly of you."

A full body flush hit me again then, and dammit he saw, because he grinned wider. Being a redhead meant that my fair skin flushed at the slightest chance, and now I knew I would never be able to conceal my thoughts around him.

I changed the subject. "Let's go to dinner, shall we?"

He nodded. "We shall."

Extending his arm, he hooked mine into the crook

of his elbow and then looked back at Piper. "Best you come along, we don't want the rumor mill starting that Madelynn and I actually like each other," Lucien told her.

Piper grinned at the king. "A love marriage would be a scandal," she agreed as she tucked her book under her arm and walked a few feet behind us.

I loved that he got along with Piper. I loved that he was saying sinfully sexy things to me at every turn, and I loved that he'd taken my advice to heart and agreed to apologize tonight at dinner. The more I got to know Lucien Thorne, the more I loved.

OH HADES. When we stepped into the dining hall my stomach dropped. It wasn't an intimate dinner with Marcelle and a few of his closest advisors. There were over a hundred courtiers in here, and each and every one was sending a frosty glare at Lucien.

He did this on purpose.

Prince Haze invited as many people as possible to make Lucien and I feel alienated.

I turned to Lucien before Prince Haze could reach us. "I didn't realize there would be so many people. You don't have to go ahead with the planned apology in front of so many."

Lucien looked out across the room and then back to me. "No. It's okay. I think you're right. My silence and space have done more harm than intended. The more the better, so that Marcelle cannot change my words with rumors."

I swallowed hard, nerves clenching my gut. He was right. More witnesses meant less chance of a rumor changing his words, but also more people who could heckle him.

Marcelle had reached us and I plastered a smile on my face.

"My king." Marcelle's voice was thick with disdain as he bowed minimally to Lucien.

"Marcelle." Lucien dropped the title from his name, and of course did not return the bow.

Marcelle looked annoyed but brushed it off. "Princess Madelynn, a pleasure." He bowed to me, his earlier flirtiness gone. He wouldn't dare try that in front of Lucien. "Come have a seat, let's celebrate your betrothal." Marcelle pointed to two empty chairs at the main table in the middle of the room.

There were seven tables in all, each one holding ten to twenty people. The tables were filled with an assortment of food and drink and everyone was chatting animatedly. I was shocked he'd been able to put on such a large dinner last minute.

"I would like a third seat for my lady-in-waiting." I

gestured to Piper, who stood beside me. She hated these events and she would kill me if I forced her to sit all night next to a bunch of people she didn't know.

"Of course." Prince Marcelle kindly asked a woman to move seats, and then Lucien, Piper, and I took our chairs.

Lucien sat at the head of the table, a place protocol dictated he take. I sat to his left, with Piper next to me, and Marcelle sat to his right across from me.

We were served an elegant meal of glazed duck and roasted yams, but it was hard for me to enjoy the food. I kept sneaking nervous glances at Lucien, wondering when he was going to give his public apology. If he was nervous, it didn't show. He sat with a straight back, gazing stonily at the people around him with little emotion.

"When is the wedding?" Marcelle asked.

Lucien's gaze flicked to the Summer prince. "Well now, that depends on if I have to deal with your little separation, now doesn't it?" Lucien said under his breath, just loud enough for Marcelle and I to hear.

Marcelle popped a chunk of sweet potato into his mouth and chewed, watching Lucien like a hawk watched a snake. "Oh, you will have to deal with it. Quite soon too. But I hope we can remain allies—"

Lucien's dinner fork stabbed his yam violently, causing the plate to crack in half. He let go of the handle, the fork sticking up straight as people looked over at him to see what the commotion was about.

Lucien then leaned forward, into Marcelle. "You will separate my kingdom over my dead body, Marcelle."

Marcelle grinned. "That can be arranged too."

I gasped at the treasonous comment. The temperature in the room dropped suddenly.

No. No. No.

This wasn't going to endear the Summer people to the winter king. Reaching under the table, I dragged my hand across Lucien's thigh and squeezed it. The coldness in the air left us quickly and he turned to face me.

"Is there something you wanted to say, sugar plum?" he asked sweetly.

Marcelle glared at Lucien and the endearing way in which he spoke to me.

"Actually, I thought now might be a good time for you to give a speech. It's been a long time since the people of Summer have seen their king." I gave a nervous laugh.

Now or never. He needed to apologize or we were better off leaving the dinner early. I pleaded with him with my eyes, then a warm hand brushed over mine, reminding me that I was still clutching his thigh. His fingers stroked the top of mine and I forgot to breathe.

Releasing his thigh, I pulled my hand back, swallowing hard, and Lucien grinned.

Clearing his throat, he stood and grabbed his spoon, clanging it against his glass. Everyone quieted, looking over at him.

My hands reached under the table to find Piper's and we clutched each other tightly, knowing what was coming.

Lucien gave a winning smile to the room, which only increased his handsomeness, and cleared his throat. "Thank you to Prince Haze and the people of Summer Court for celebrating my betrothal to Princess Madelynn."

Everyone clapped politely and then went back to eating. Lucien cleared his throat louder and everyone quieted again, looking over at him with furrowed brows. Lucien gazed at me. "My future queen has already made a lasting impression on me and made me want to be a better man. To right my wrongs..." he said, and my heart constricted. Piper squeezed my hand and I gripped hers right back.

Who knew that Lucien Thorne would be the most romantic man I'd ever met?

"The truth is, I made a mistake in being silent and staying away all these years since the Great Freeze," he stated, and people started to murmur to each other.

"What is he doing?" Marcelle whispered to me. I ignored him.

"I made a mistake," Lucien said. "It was an accident that I greatly regret. Not a night passes that I don't have to live with the remorse. I am sorry." He held his hand over his heart and glanced out at the room. Tears filled my eyes at his heartfelt apology. It was much more than I had expected and anyone could see how genuine it was.

The murmurs grew louder, and finally an older woman stood and pointed at him. "Accidents with controlling your magic happen, but you didn't even send a letter explaining why. I buried my husband," she roared, "and now I have to bow to his killer just because he is my king!"

I gasped at the woman's sharp words. Lucien flinched as if they'd cut him. A few others murmured their agreements, and pretty soon the entire room was shouting at the king.

Oh Maker, this was not what I'd intended.

I peered at Marcelle, who looked positively delighted with the turn of events, and panic started to rise up in me.

The winter king stepped away from the table and walked over to the woman as every single person in the room went stock still.

Don't hurt her, I prayed to the Maker. I didn't

know Lucien well enough to tell what he would do. But he did have a temper and she'd just screamed at him. I was clenching Piper's hand so tightly that it probably hurt, but I couldn't move.

When Lucien finally stood before the woman, we all watched in fear for what he might do. Marcelle's fingers twitched as if he was ready to use magic against his own king any moment.

But what Lucien did next caused the tears to spill over onto my cheeks.

He knelt before her, resting on his knee and bowing his head deeply. "I bow to you now, my lady. Please accept my humble apology. I was a young boy with too much power and no control. I didn't think in your grief that you would want to hear the excuses of that young boy in a letter, or to see his face, so I just stayed away."

The woman's bottom lip quivered as she stared down at the winter king kneeling on one knee before her. She looked to be in shock. Her eyes misted over and she swallowed hard.

After a few moments, she tapped his shoulder. He glanced up at her and then she leaned in and whispered something in his ear. I couldn't hear it from here, but it caused him to rise, and they embraced.

It was a beautiful moment, the best I could have

hoped for, and I wished he'd done the same in my court and in Spring.

I looked over at Piper and smiled.

"No!" Marcelle slammed his fist on the table, causing my glass to fall over and gush water on my plate. Marcelle stood, and the room was suddenly sweltering with heat. "You're going to listen to the carefully orchestrated lies of this madman!" Marcelle screamed to his people. "He admits he lost control. You want to follow a king who can't even control his power? What happens the next time he gets mad? We have an eternal winter? More die!" Some of the Summer people nodded in agreement, but the majority kept silent.

Lucien looked like he'd been slapped. Here he was giving a genuine apology, confronting his demons, which I'd asked him to do, and Marcelle was twisting it.

"He's not my king," Marcelle said boldly, and tipped his chin high.

That's when a torrent of rage exploded within me.

"How dare you!" I shouted, standing so fast that the chair I had been sitting in fell backwards. The window at the far end of the room shattered and a strong wind burst into the room, throwing all of the flowers and light cloth napkins into the air. People gasped and watched in shock as I pulled a small wind tunnel around Marcelle. "You will not disrespect the king like that and live," I declared. "What you have said is treason! You have forgotten your place, Marcelle Haze!"

My words mixed with the wind, making them sound thunderous as they moved around the room. Marcelle looked genuinely terrified, realizing he'd gone too far. It made me wonder how often he spoke like this, to let it slip before the king himself. This was the making of an uprising. No wonder he wanted to separate the realms. The difference between Lucien and I was that I had complete control over my power. This little display was on purpose, and I wanted every single person present to know it. The wind funnel followed Marcelle as he backed up, his hair and clothing being tossed around him.

"Kneel and pledge your loyalty to Lucien Thorne, king of Winter, leader of Thorngate and of all fae," I seethed, "or I will tear the skin from your body layer by layer."

Gasps of shock filled the room. I no longer cared that this wasn't proper behavior for a lady. Lucien wasn't perfect but he *was* our leader, our king, and to disrespect him in front of a room of courtiers like that was not something I would stand for. Lucien suddenly appeared beside me, standing before Marcelle.

I had no idea what he thought of my current

behavior and I didn't care. Marcelle would kneel or I was well within my right to prosecute him for treason.

Marcelle looked to me, then to the king, and he fell to one knee, bowing his head deeply. Relief rushed through me and I stopped the wind all at once and it became eerily silent.

"Forgive me, King. I drank too much wine and forgot my place," Marcelle said, his voice shaking a little. He'd had no wine.

Lucien stared at Marcelle on his knee, head bowed, and said nothing for a full minute. It was as if he was soaking the moment in. No one in the room moved. We were all waiting to hear the fate of the man who'd just spoken such treasonous words.

"You may rise and keep your life," Lucien said, and the courtiers around us sighed in relief.

I was angry for a moment with that decision, but then I realized Lucien was playing a longer game here, to win the hearts of the Summer Court. If he had killed Marcelle it would have squashed the separation petition, but an uprising would happen eventually. They would hate him even more.

Lucien turned to the crowd and then looked at me. "I'm quite a lucky man, am I not? To have a woman fight for respect on my behalf?"

The room chuckled nervously at the topic change and the tension broke. Some women smiled adoringly at us, and the men nodded their agreement with Lucien. Then Lucien hooked arms with mine. "We will leave you now, but we hope to see you at our wedding." We both spun, and together walked quickly out of the room, with Piper trailing behind.

My heart was in my throat the entire walk through the palace. There were servants down every hallway so I couldn't say a word or ask him anything in private. I was nearly shaking by the time we reached his front doorstep tucked into the garden with the night sky around us.

Would he be mad? Had I completely overstepped? Did he hate me for sticking up for him when he so clearly could do it himself? Had I made him look weak?

Piper was in the garden sitting on the bench under the moonlight, and we were finally alone. I looked up at Lucien, hoping he would just say something, anything. But he just watched me with those stormy gray eyes.

"My king, I'm sorry if—" My words were cut off when his lips pressed against mine. I gasped and he swallowed the sound. His hands came up to cup my face and my shock gave way to desire. My lips parted and he inserted his tongue, causing me to moan. One second I was standing in front of the door and then next he spun, moving me so that my back was pressed *against* the door. His thumb trailed down my neck as our tongues stroked each other. Heat traveled down my chest and settled between my legs. I never wanted this kiss to stop. It was raw and full of passion, in a way I'd never felt before outside of my beloved romance novels.

This kiss said *I approve of what you did.*

It said *I appreciate you.*

It said *thank you.*

It said *so* much more.

Kissing a man like Lucien Thorne was nothing like kissing the boys behind school. This kiss promised that one day when we bedded, there would be more where that came from. There would be pleasure for both of us.

When he finally pulled back, I was panting. I hated that he'd stopped, but also I was grateful. I was not sure I ever would have, and Piper was a rule breaker, so she would let it go on forever. But if we were seen it would tarnish my reputation and he knew that.

He was lightly holding my throat, his lips glistening with my saliva when he leaned in and whispered into my ear: "Had I known you kissed like that, I would have doubled your dowry."

I grinned at the compliment as he pulled away from me.

"Well, goodnight," I said stupidly, my mind still on his tongue and how he tasted and smelled and felt.

I turned to go get Piper for our walk back to our room.

"Madelynn," he called, and I spun to face him, still breathless. "Would you have killed Marcelle?"

His question shocked me, but not more than the answer. Lucien had poured his heart out in front of a room full of strangers. He'd humbled himself before that widow and bowed to her. And Marcelle ruined it.

"Yes," I said honestly, and then turned before I could see the response on his face.

I didn't want to know if he was disappointed or delighted with my answer. Though I believed I knew Lucien well enough now to know it was the latter.

7

We got out of Summer Court before the sun had even risen. Things going down with Marcelle last night were not good, so if there were a true rebellion we could be in trouble. I'd barely slept, replaying that kiss over and over in my head. It was like we'd been made for each other, fitting together perfectly, our tongues dancing to the same song. Piper kept asking me to describe the kiss and swooning as she fell back on the couch clutching her romance novel.

"You're Elowyn," she would say, and we would start to giggle.

Now we rode for Winter Court. It would be nearly a full day's journey having to cross through the corner of Spring Court and then into Winter to parade through town. Lucien took turns sitting in the carriage with me for a few hours while I read, and then riding on horseback with his soldiers for a bit while I talked to Piper.

When we were nearly to the Winter Court border, the smell of smoke filtered through the carriage and I popped my head out to see a fire in the distance.

Our little caravan had stopped, and Lucien was speaking with his soldiers.

"Could be a trap to lure us over there," his lead guardsman said.

I slipped out of the caravan and stepped onto the highest stair, looking at the flames touching the top of the building. It was a farmhouse and it was on fire.

"Are we in Spring?" I asked, noticing the beautiful flowers and damp earth.

Lucien turned back to me. "Yes, so either that fae doesn't have much power to make it rain, or it's a trick."

"You can freeze people where they stand and I can pull the breath from their lungs. What are we waiting for, let's go offer help. If it's a trick, we kill them," I said plainly.

Lucien looked to his lead guard with a raised

eyebrow and then at me. "Have I mentioned how much I love your secretly violent nature?"

I scoffed. "I'm not violent!"

Lucien kicked his horse lightly and it turned around, coming to my side. "Well then, Princess, let's go see what we can do to help or hurt these people."

Well, when he put it like that, it *did* sound violent. I merely meant that if it were a trick, we could easily overpower the bandits.

I lowered myself onto his horse, sitting sidesaddle and then slipping my arms around his waist. I tried not to focus on the hard muscle beneath my fingers or the fresh pine smell of his hair. I really tried not to remember the way he tasted, like mint and honey.

Piper cleared her throat behind us. I turned and she was staring at Lucien's lead guard. "I'd like to accompany," she said.

The guard looked to Lucien, who nodded once.

Piper protected my modesty like it was the last piece of chocolate cake. And the piece now had Lucien's name on it. The very thought caused a blush to climb up my cheeks and distracted me from the task at hand. By the time my thoughts were back with the smoke, we'd reached the fire.

"Oh Hades!" I cursed when I saw a single old fae who looked about seventy winters aged. He had a bucket and was scooping it into the horse trough and trying to put out the fire that lapped up the side of his house. I could see now he'd had a burn pit off to the side, trying to burn some trash, and it had gotten out of hand.

Without thinking, I jumped off the horse and landed hard on the balls of my feet. A stinging sensation rang up the backs of my heels but I ignored it.

Throwing my arms out, I pulled the air from the fire, causing the flames to half in size. Lucien was right behind me, pulling clouds from the sky over our little area and then the temperature dropped.

It was at this moment that the man realized he was not alone. He turned to look at us and Piper ran to him. "Is anyone in the house?" she asked frantically.

The man stared at us in shock. "No, my wife went to town. My trash burn pit got out of control."

"Keep him warm!" Lucien snapped, and then white fluff dumped from the sky. Lucien couldn't make it rain like a Spring fae could, but he could extract the rain from the clouds and freeze it. Piper grasped the old man's shoulders and pulled him away from the flurry as I stepped closer to Lucien. Using my power, I guided the large chunks of falling snow onto the flames. They cracked and snapped as they hit the hot fire, but the amount Lucien was dumping was overwhelming the blaze. Together we worked without saying a word and put out the fire on the side of the man's house. Afterward, I glanced over at Lucien and he was watching me keenly.

"You and I work well together," I murmured, and his entire face lifted into a devastatingly handsome smile.

"We do," he agreed.

I couldn't help but match his grin. Being around this man made me happy. I never would have thought that a few days ago.

"I'm going to go inside and blow any smoke out," I told him.

He nodded. "I'll come."

I knew it was for protection, which was sweet, but it should have been clear to him now that I could take care of myself.

Stepping inside, I coughed when I was met with a large plume of thick smoke. Sucking the wind through the cracked open window at the kitchen, I blew all the smoke out the front door in a matter of minutes. When we were done, Lucien and I stepped inside to assess the damage.

The wall was miraculously still standing, with only the inside corner of the dining room burnt and open to the outside.

"With light repairs, he and his wife can remain here," I said.

Lucien was looking at some pictures on the wall.

"I'll see to it that Duke Barrett provides the necessary help for him."

I stepped over to him, reaching out to touch one of the pictures. In one stood the old man and who I assumed to be his wife, but they looked thirty years younger. She was holding a small purple flower and he held a shovel. They were both grinning as they stood in an open field.

"They look happy," I observed.

Lucien inclined his head to me. "Love will do that to people."

"Reminds me of my parents." I smiled. "My father is obsessed with my mother. It's adorable and sickening."

Lucien laughed. "They sound lucky to me."

"What was your parents' marriage like?" I wondered aloud. I knew that when his mother died, his father, who was king at the time, had rightfully taken it hard. He abdicated and no one had seen or heard from him since. Lucien had been the public head of the Thorne household since then.

A shadow crossed over his face, his eyes growing stormy. "We should head outside and make sure the old man is okay."

He stepped away from me and I deflated a little. Lucien had so many touchy topics, I felt like I was constantly dancing around them. Still, he was opening up to me little by little, so I wasn't going to push him.

Two things were off the conversation table, the cause of the Great Freeze and his parents.

I stepped outside, following after Lucien, and took in the scene before me.

"Bless you, King Thorne." The man was weeping as he clung to Lucien's arm.

Lucien looked uncomfortable with this display of emotion, unsure what to do, so he just stood there rigidly. I wanted to laugh at the sight. It was sweet and comical. But I didn't think Lucien would appreciate that much.

"Let's get you inside and warm," I told the old man, pulling him away from Lucien, who looked relieved.

Piper and I got the old man settled inside, and Lucien sent one of his guards to Spring Court with word to send help for the old man and his wife.

Once we all settled back into the carriage, I felt good about what we'd done.

ONLY A FEW HOURS LATER, a chill rushed through the carriage. I realized then that we were in Winter Court. Lucien appeared suddenly with two fur cloaks, handing one to Piper and then another to me.

Mine was white rabbit fur and Piper's was a reddish brown, probably fox.

"Gifts from me to you," he said casually, like it wasn't a sweet and thoughtful thing that had my heart racing.

Piper looked at me in shock. The king did not usually get expensive gifts for ladies in waiting. But because Piper was important to me, he'd made her important to him.

"This is very sweet," I told him, slipping it over my shoulders. The warmth immediately enveloped me and I relaxed. Truth be told, I loved winter. Snow was magical, as was sledding and all of the other fun things you could do. Did I like it year-round? I supposed we would see.

When the clapping started, I realized we'd already entered the gates.

Pulling back the curtain, I opened the window and reached out to the people. They were smiling joyously, grasping my hand and running alongside the carriage.

"Our future queen!" the children shouted as they ran, and a light snow began to fall. I looked across the carriage at Lucien, who was watching me with a smile.

Something fluttered in my chest, and I realized that I had so wrongly judged this man. He was kind, intelligent, protective and... flawed. But weren't we all? He had a temper, but never with me. There was a line in my favorite romance novel that said, *He only had eyes for me*. Oh how I'd longed to be that girl when I'd first read that line.

And now, as I looked across at Lucien peering at me, I thought that maybe I was.

I returned his smile and reached out to grasp his hand. He took mine and we interlaced our fingers under the carriage window so that no one saw. With our free hands, we waved to his people who packed the street so thickly that we could barely get through.

It was by far the greatest reception we'd had. He was a beloved king in his own realm.

The fake rumors to make him feared didn't hold up here, I thought.

When we finally reached the Winter palace, I looked up at the stone structure—my new home. It was bigger than I remembered. As a little girl I'd come here with my parents and some other royals a few times, but I never really remembered Lucien. He always stayed out of sight or with the other realms' princes, who were now kings.

The massive white stone looked as if it were carved from ice, and I shivered a little at the chill in the air.

When we stepped out of the carriage, Lucien looked at the palace with a haunted expression. I frowned, wondering why returning home would cause him to look that way. Didn't he love it here? Was it memories of his mother?

My teeth started to chatter and Lucien shook himself. "Let's get you inside by the fire," he said, placing a hand on my lower back and waving to his people as we passed. The snow was falling in clumps now and I wondered if it was because Lucien was anxious. Winter didn't always need to be frigid and snowy, but this realm was greatly tied to his emotions, and I wondered now what had him on edge.

Piper pulled her fur coat around her as Lucien's lead servant bowed deeply to us both. "Your Highness, welcome home," he said and then looked to me. "Princess Madelynn, we are all overjoyed at the announcement of your betrothal."

I smiled warmly at him and thanked him as he ushered us inside. The warmth of a fire rushed at me and I sighed in relief as I slipped out of my now snow-covered shoes and walked over to the gigantic drawing room hearth. The stone chimney rose up over three stories high and made for a beautiful conversation piece. While Piper and I warmed our hands, Lucien gave orders to his staff to have my things brought to my wing of the house and for dinner to be heated. It had been a long, cold day, and when I heard him say the words "meat stew," my mouth watered.

After giving the instructions, Lucien came to join

us at the fire. He was watching me nervously. "Do you like the palace? You can redecorate if you want. These are all things my mother picked out and—"

"It's beautiful," I told him with a smile.

It was. Silver, gold, gray and white. It was like Winter Solstice Festival year-round. I wouldn't mind eventually bringing in some color, but it was nicely done. The highbacked chairs looked to be carved from oak and stained a rich black.

"Is this her?" a deep, gravelly voice slurred from behind me, and I startled a little.

Spinning, I gazed upon a tall man with an overgrown beard. He wore a simple white tunic with stains along the front, and he clutched a bottle of wine. For a second I thought he was a vagrant, until Lucien stiffened beside me.

"Father, I told you I would get you when we were ready for dinner." Lucien's voice held a high-pitched tone full of anxiety.

Father? This was the old King Thorne? My heart hammered in my chest as he shuffled forward, bumping into the chair as he tried to make his way to me.

He was clearly drunk.

Looking me up and down, he nodded. "Not bad." Then he looked at Lucien. "And she agreed to marry your sorry arse?"

I gasped a little and glanced at Lucien, but he was devoid of all emotion.

"She did," he said flatly.

The old king stared at me and squinted. "He's worthless. Couldn't even save his own mother."

My mouth popped open in shock. I expected Lucien to tear across the room, to maybe even grab his father by the throat. I waited for it to start snowing, anything to show he was mad, but Lucien's shoulders just slumped and his head hung.

I looked at Piper, unsure what to do. She shrugged, eyes wide. If it were anyone else I would give them a piece of my mind, but this was his father, the former king.

I decided then to treat him as I would a child who misbehaved. When Libby wanted attention, she sometimes did naughty things. If you ignored her, she stopped.

Slipping my hand into Lucien's, I looked up at him. "I hear you have a wonderful library. Would you show me?"

His father started to mumble something else but I pulled Lucien away from him, Piper trailing far behind us now. We traversed the halls until we reached a set of double doors.

Lucien opened them, and the collective intake of breath that Piper and I took then did no justice to the space. It was two stories high, floor-to-ceiling with shelves, three rolling ladders, and over a thousand books at least!

Piper gravitated towards one book as Lucien turned to face me.

"I'm sorry about my father... I should have told you. I was going to but..." He trailed off.

I gave him a sweet smile. "It's okay."

I wouldn't lie. Seeing the old king in such a state had been a shock, but who didn't have that one embarrassing family member? I was hoping his cruelness to Lucien was a one-time thing I had just witnessed and would not continue. Wine and moonshine did horrible things to men who couldn't control their lust of it. What his father had just said out there was proof.

"You know you're not at fault for your mother's death, right? You couldn't have saved her. You're not a healing elf," I said suddenly, wondering if he believed his father.

He sighed, looking distant and withdrawn. "I don't know anything about that anymore. He's said it so many times, I'm starting to wonder if it's true."

My heart dropped into my stomach then and I reached for him, but he backed away. "I should consult with my staff. I've been away a while. I'll see you at dinner?"

Unshed tears were lining my eyes, and Lucien's

form blurred, so I just nodded and he left me in the library. I blinked rapidly to clear my vision, and Piper ran to my side.

"Did you hear that?" I asked her. She looked distraught, so I thought maybe she had.

She nodded, staring at the closed door. "Do you think that's why he doesn't drink?"

I gasped. Yes, it all made sense. Lucien didn't have the problem, his father did, and probably in an effort to not have an issue himself, Lucien widely stayed away from wine and mead.

"It's just proof that you don't really know what a person is going through in their private life and we shouldn't be quick to judge them based on rumors," Piper said.

I nodded, slinging my arm around her shoulders. "You're too wise for your years, Piper. Too wise indeed."

She smiled and we exited the library to go in search of my rooms... in the place I would soon be calling home. It was overwhelming and exciting all at once. Mostly because now that I had kissed Lucien, I was one hundred percent sure that I wanted to marry him. I couldn't imagine not ever kissing those lips again. Who said that arranged marriages couldn't also become love marriages?

The rooms that had been designated for me were bigger than what I'd had at the Fall Court palace. I had a private bedroom, three guest quarters, a sitting room for tea, three washrooms, and my own library! Not to mention servant quarters for Piper, and a small kitchen. It was like my own little house in a wing of the castle shared with the king and his father. I had no idea what type of living arrangements we would do after we were married. Most arranged marriages started with separate bedrooms, and the couple only came together for the occasional bedding to make an heir. I wasn't sure if Lucien would want to keep to himself and I would always have this side of the castle or what. The thought of it made me a little lonely.

After getting cleaned up and changed, I slipped into a silver gown with white fur trim and walked down to dinner with Piper.

On the way, some courtiers popped into the hallway to greet us and introduce themselves. We met Master Greeves, who was the head of the household staff, and the one I should go to with any issues. Then we were greeted by a delightful older woman who was the baker and palace chef, Mrs. Pennyworth.

We also met a few high-ranking soldiers, some housekeepers, and a palace healing elf, and I was highly impressed with everyone. They were respectful and seemed genuinely excited to have a new queen. I felt very welcome, and the evil rumors about this place fell flat.

When I entered the dining hall, I was disappointed to see Lucien's father, Vincent sitting at the table holding a glass of wine and glaring at his son.

I had hoped it would be just us, and that his father would go sleep off his drunkenness somewhere. Maybe he was like this all the time? Was this normal for them? I shuddered to think it. I had never seen my father this drunk. It was improper, especially of royalty.

"Mr. Thorne." I curtsied to him. "Wonderful to see you again."

He looked at his son. "You don't deserve her," he said, and my spine went rigid.

Lucien's jaw clenched and he waved his butler over. "We can be served now."

Lucien was just going to ignore that ugly comment? I felt a little sick at how verbally abusive Lucien's father was being and he was doing nothing about it. It was a far cry from the hot-tempered man I had just spent a few days on the road with.

Lucien sat at the head of the table with his father to his left. I sat on Lucien's right with Piper next to me.

"Do you like your living quarters?" Lucien asked me as a hot steaming stew was placed before me.

I nodded. "They're lovely. Very large. I might get a little lonely. It's bigger than anything I had at the Fall Court palace."

Lucien's eyes hooded over. "Well it's only until we are married. Then you will be joining me in my rooms, right?"

I nearly choked on my stew. I couldn't believe he said that in front of his father. But I also was excited at the prospect that he didn't want the typical arranged marriage and separate rooms.

"Right." I laughed nervously.

Piper was grinning. I kicked her lightly under the table.

Lucien's dad hadn't eaten any of his soup. Instead, he upended the wine cup into his mouth and then stared at me. "Why would you marry him?" he asked with a stony expression.

"Father, stop it," Lucien said under his breath.

"Don't tell me what to do!" his father snapped, flicking his hand towards his son. An icicle shot from his palm and cut into the side of Lucien's face before crashing into the wall behind him.

I gasped, waiting for Lucien to retaliate. But he didn't. He just pulled a napkin to his cheek and hung his head in embarrassment.

This happens all the time.

The thought horrified me. I wanted to take my knife and cut his father's cheek in retaliation, but I knew that was insane. I'd never felt this protective over someone. The king was more powerful than I was and didn't need my protection normally, but... it seemed with his father he did. This man had abused him before; otherwise Lucien wouldn't be so docile.

Since he was a child? I didn't know. Definitely since his mother died. Lucien had stopped fighting for whatever reason.

I stood and his father tracked my movements. Walking over to Lucien, I tipped his chin up to look him in the eyes. I wasn't prepared to stare into the gaze of a small, wounded boy. It gutted me, and a fresh wave of anger rushed through me. "I'd like to eat dinner with you alone," I told him. "Do you have a smaller dining room?"

Lucien's face relaxed into my hand and the scared little boy retreated. "I do." He stood, grabbing his bowl of stew.

Piper grabbed our bowls and we walked to the huge open doors of the large dining hall.

His father's scoff sounded behind us and I turned to look back at him. He was glaring at me now.

"You may join us for dinners when you are sober," I informed him, and we left the room.

It was a silent walk down the hall. A few of Lucien's wait staff followed us in confusion. Lucien led us into a small dining room with just two seats and a small round table. There was a huge window on the far wall that overlooked the magnificent snow-covered fields behind the palace.

I glanced at Piper after she set my bowl down, and she waved me off. "I'll be in the corner."

One of Lucien's staff grabbed a chair and small standing tray for Piper, and she sat in the corner of the room, eating alone. I felt bad for her, but after Lucien and I were married she wouldn't need to follow me around like this. It was to protect my reputation, I knew, but it felt silly at times, especially times like these when I wanted so badly to have a private conversation with him.

Lucien sat next to me, eating his stew quietly and staring out at the falling snow. It was coming down in clumps and looked magical.

"I quite like this room. I think we should take all of our meals in here," I told him.

He gave me a sad smile and it broke my heart. We ate in silence, and I couldn't help but replay what had happened with his father over and over again.

"I'm embarrassed you had to see that," Lucien finally managed to say. "I'm sorry... I wish he would just die already, or go live in the mountains and leave me be."

I swallowed hard, but didn't judge his harsh words, not after what I'd just seen. "Has he always done that sort of thing?"

Lucien shrugged. "Not so much when my mother was alive, but a lot after she passed. He doesn't remember the next day."

Not so much. That wasn't the answer I wanted. And not remembering was no excuse. It reminded me of the elder in our court who'd had a drinking problem and needed help.

Reaching out, I grasped his hand. "Why don't you stand up to him?" I'd seen him lose his temper with others a dozen times over the past days. But with his father it was like he was dead inside.

Lucien gave me a haunting look, his eyes dull and void of emotion. "Because the last time I did I froze the entire realm for a full day and night."

I gasped. That was the reason for the Great Freeze? He'd gotten in a fight with his father and couldn't control his power? His father must have beaten him, told him he was responsible for his mother's death because he didn't save her. What did those words do to an innocent sixteen-year-old boy who was already hurting inside?

"Oh, Lu—"

He stood, scooting his chair backwards abruptly. "I'm exhausted from the day's travel. I'll turn in and see you in the morning."

I was so stunned by his revelation that all I could do was nod. His father had pushed him too far that night and now he was afraid to stand up for himself for fear of freezing the realm again. Over fifty people died that night. He felt fear at causing such a thing again.

Well, I wasn't afraid. I had complete control over my power. I stood abruptly and Piper ran to my side. "Don't do anything crazy," she warned, knowing me too well.

She'd heard everything Lucien had just said. I looked at her with what I hoped was an unhinged expression. "You told me to stick up for my man, to show Lucien what it would be like to have a supportive queen by his side."

Piper's eyes widened. "Yeah, well, that was in relation to Marcelle, not the former winter king!" she whisper-screamed.

She was worried for me after seeing his display of power when he cut Lucien's cheek with the icicle, but I didn't fear that man. Ice could be turned to snow with one gust of wind.

I tipped my chin high. "I will *not* live in this home without that man being put in his place."

Piper looked worriedly at the doorway, her mind no doubt churning through protocols and decorum.

"Wait here," I told her. "Best there are no witnesses. Then it's my word against that of a drunken fool."

Her mouth popped open and I blasted past her, going in search of the man with the black heart who called himself a father.

I FOUND Vincent Thorne in the dining room where I had left him. His wine glass was full and his soup barely touched. His beard was so long it dipped into the soup and it almost made me feel sorry for him.

Almost.

There was no staff here, so I closed the doors behind me after I entered. He looked up at the sound to see me and rolled his eyes.

"Go away and leave a man in peace," he snapped.

"No," I growled. I didn't care if it was inappropriate, I didn't care what protocol dictated, I would not allow him to bully Lucien and I, and whatever children we would have, for the rest of our lives.

I looked up at the small circle window at the top of the far wall and pulled my power to me, making a small crack in the glass and generating enough wind to make my hair blow around and let Vincent know I was pissed.

Lucien's father laughed then, a drunken, grating sound. "I made her mad!" he cackled to no one.

I calmly strode over to Vincent and stood before him, gathering more wind with me and using it to press him into his chair. His eyes widened.

"You would dare use your power against me!?" he roared, and the temperature in the room plunged.

I leaned forward, hoping I looked as venomous as I felt. "I *would*. In fact, if you ever draw blood on Lucien again, I will *kill* you."

His mouth popped open in shock. He struggled against my invisible hold but I detained him firmly in place.

"And from now on, if you want to be in your son's, or my presence, you will be sober."

"You don't tell me what to do!" Lucien's father snarled, frost crawling along the walls around me. I pushed more wind at him so that the very skin on his face was shaking and flapping against my power.

Then I leaned forward, pressing a finger to his chest, pushing enough wind into him that it made him struggle to breathe. It was a dark side of my power, something we did a thousand times a day and didn't really think about. Breathing. And I had control of it all. I could take the air from his lungs without leaving a trace. "Your son is king. You abdicated, *remember*? And soon *I* will be your queen. That puts my station above yours. I'm sorry for the loss of your wife but it's no excuse for this behavior. She would no doubt be ashamed of you. I will not bring children into a home with a grandfather like you."

He looked stricken, like I'd finally broken through the icy shell that encased his dead heart. Then his face turned into a menacing snarl. "You're just as bad as Lucien!" he roared, and I felt the frost claw at my ankles. "A dirty little whore who—"

I'd had enough. With one thought I *pulled* the air from his lungs and his eyes bulged in fear.

I grinned in his face, ignoring the freezing of my feet. He was drunk and didn't have enough power to defeat me. "Oh, Lucien honey," I mocked, in a devastated voice, "I don't know what happened. Your father just stopped breathing. I think the wine weakened his heart."

Vincent's eyes bugged even wider, his face turning purple.

"Maybe I should just end you right now," I mused. I didn't know what had come over me. It was like all of the repressed anger I'd been carrying my entire life was unleashing in this moment. I had to be perfect and proper Madelynn, the eldest, the most powerful, I had to do as I was told. I didn't want to do as I was told anymore. I wanted to kill this bastard and save the man I was pretty sure I was falling in love with from having to ever be hurt by him again.

"I'm sorry." He mouthed the words, unable to speak. His frost and coldness fell away all at once and I realized that I had gone too far. Killing Lucien's father wasn't the answer. Maybe this piece of trash could still be saved.

I dropped my power and Vincent fell forward onto his hands and knees, gasping for air. He beat on his chest and I watched, waiting for his response. It would determine his fate.

When he finally caught his breath, he got up and sat back in the chair. He then reached for the wine bottle next to his glass.

I caught his arm with my hand and he looked into my eyes. Lucien had said something to me at dinner that I now knew he'd never have the courage to tell his father. So I was going to do it for him. "You cannot live here like this. The elves have a healing technique that helps with this. You can spend a few weeks there and they get you sober. Take away the urge."

Fear flashed in his gaze and I realized he was scared of going without it, of not having wine and mead at his fingertips to drown his pain and anger—or whatever reason he drank.

I shrugged. "Or you can move to a cottage in the mountains. I will send provisions, enough wine and mead to drink yourself to death."

His mouth popped open in shock. I knew that no one had ever spoken to him so boldly. Maybe that was the problem. This pathetic excuse for a man had gone unchecked for too long.

"Your choice, *Vincent.*" I used his first name to hopefully cut him deeper.

"You're... you're..." He seemed at a loss for words. I dared him to call me a *whore* or any other foul name again.

He sighed, falling back into his chair and rubbing his chest. "Fine, I'll try the elf place, and if it doesn't work, or I don't like it, I'll take the cottage in the mountains. Have the wine ready for me," he grumbled, and crossed his arms like a sour-faced child.

I nodded, relieved he didn't try to pick a fight again.

The lack of drink for the past ten minutes seemed to have slightly sobered him. He stared off into the distance. I wasn't sure how to leave this conversation but I wasn't going to apologize.

"You're right," he said, his voice hollow as a tear slid down his cheek. "My wife would be ashamed of me."

I nodded in agreement. "Then shape up, so Lucien and I don't have to be."

His mouth set into a grim line at that, but he nodded once, more tears flowing.

The tears I wasn't prepared for. Did he feel regret for how he treated Lucien or was this part of the drunkenness? Or did he only miss his wife? I was waffling between wanting to smack him and hug him. So I decided it was time I go.

"I'll arrange your stay at the elvin sober infirmary," I told him and let myself out of the room.

When I opened the door, a yelp left my throat as I came face to face with Lucien. He stared wide-eyed into the room at his father and then at me.

Oh fae.

Did he hear everything? Or just the last part. He

looked... scared, and angry, and... something else. This wasn't like with Marcelle when I'd stuck up for him. This was with his own father and I knew I'd hugely overstepped.

I closed the door behind me and found myself standing in the dimly lit hallway alone with Lucien Thorne. His eyes glowed a dark gray as a chill swept through the corridor, causing a shiver to run up my spine.

It was improper to be seen without a chaperone. If household staff caught us, they could start rumors. But I didn't care. I cared more about what he heard me say and what he thought.

"I'm sorry for butting into your private family matters," I began as he watched me with those glowing eyes, a storm no doubt raging inside. "But if I am to be queen, your wife, the mother of your children, I must feel safe in my own home."

His chest heaved and he seemingly fought for breath. I swallowed hard, unable to read his reaction so I went on. "Your father and I have spoken and he has agreed to attend a discreet elvin sober infirmary that I know of, and if he cannot stay off the wine he will go to the mountains and live out the rest of his life alone."

Lucien didn't move and didn't speak. I was starting to internally panic. Did he want to call off the wedding? Had I gone too far?

But when I looked at him, *really* looked at him, I could see that he was terrified. Stepping forward, I cupped his jaw in my hands. "He can't hurt you anymore. Not while I'm here," I whispered.

I didn't think Lucien was afraid of his father, he was more powerful than him, but he was afraid of himself. Lucien's power, like mine, was tied to his emotions. But I had a wonderful childhood; my emotions were stable and controlled. Lucien's were not. This fear was that if he reacted too strongly to his father, like he really wanted to, like he had all those years ago, he would kill us all, freeze us to ice. That fear was paralyzing him, and clearly had for years when it came to his father.

Leaning forward, he inched closer to me and I froze. "I'm in love with you," he breathed against my mouth, and then his lips crashed into mine. I wasn't prepared for that and so I whimpered in surprise and joy.

I kicked his father out of his home and he loved me? The things I saw as flaws and overstepping, he *loved.* I parted my lips as his tongue came to stroke against mine and then he stumbled backwards into a set of doors that swung on squeaky hinges. I opened my eyes for a second to find we were back in the library. His hand gripped my hip with an almost painful urgency and heat bloomed between my legs.

When my back hit the library bookcase, I moaned in surprise. Right now he was rough, and I liked it. This desperate need to be together only made my own passion grow. I boldly reached under his tunic and allowed my fingers to caress his bare chest muscles.

The guttural moan that came from his throat left me breathless.

This was *so* improper, *so* beyond protocols for a royal marriage, and yet... I wanted to bed him right here and now. In the library. I'd saved my purity for my wedding night and this kiss with Lucien Thorne made me want to give it up right here among these books.

My mother told me it would be a tight pinch the first time, sometimes a little blood, then a lot of pleasure if you were with a man who knew what he was doing. I had a feeling Lucien knew his way around a woman's body.

But I also wanted that night to be special, something saved for a man I loved. I had no hope of marrying for love with the knowledge that my father would one day pick a suitor for me. But now... I knew it was possible.

Pulling away from Lucien, I looked him in the eyes. "I'm in love with you too," I declared. "And we will most definitely be bedding for more than just making children."

The full-fledged grin that graced his face made my

stomach flip over. To be able to have that effect on him, it brought me great joy.

Lucien's lips were pink and swollen as he released me and smoothed his tunic. Then he let his eyes rake over my dress. "You should go before I rip that dress off of you and do something very naughty," he said, and my cheeks blushed.

Thinking of leaving him tomorrow made me suddenly sad. "Let's get married next month. I don't fancy a long betrothal," I told him boldly.

Lucien's eyes went half lidded. "No. A month is far too long. Let's marry this same day next week. I'll put my staff on overtime and everything can be ready."

My entire face lifted with a smile. "Next week it is."

Seven days to return to Fall Court, gather all my things and say goodbye to my childhood home. I would be sad to leave them, but I knew now Lucien wouldn't mind frequent visits. And now that I had a taste of what my life would be like as a married woman, I wanted it.

Now.

"Goodnight, Lucien," I told him breathlessly as I stood in the library doorway.

"Goodnight, sugar plum."

I smiled all the way back to my room.

The next morning Piper and I came down for breakfast and there was an urgency in the air. Lucien was shouting commands at a guard and the palace staff were running around in a frenzy. My mind went into panic mode. After getting to my room last night I'd written a letter to my elvin friend to arrange a stay for Lucien's father discreetly. I had given it to one of Lucien's guards to deliver. Had it somehow caused an issue?

"What's happened?" I asked.

Lucien spun when he saw me, his eyes looking a bit

frantic. He reached for the crook of my elbow and dragged me into an alcove away from the rest of the staff. "For a few weeks now some Winter Court fae have gone missing."

I nodded. "Same with Fall. We assume they ran off to Cinder Mountain."

When a person wasn't happy with their lot and wanted to leave, they always went to Cinder Mountain in Embergate. It had become a safe haven of sorts for all the different races and hybrids.

Lucien shook his head. "A week ago, one of my most powerful soldiers went missing. Then Raife, the elf king, showed up here saying that the Nightfall queen had a device that stripped a person of their magic."

I gasped. The human queen and her stupid devices! They were awful, but stripping a person of their magic? It sounded impossible and especially evil.

Lucien shook his head. "I didn't put it together until my missing soldier showed back up this morning, bloodied and half dead. *Without* his magic."

Another gasp escaped me. I was in shock, unable to speak. "That's dreadful, I'm so sorry for your soldier. You must be close."

Lucien looked positively beside himself with worry. The winter king swallowed hard, leaning in closer to me and holding my gaze. "I do feel bad for Dominik, but that's not what has me so concerned."

I frowned. "What is it?"

Lucien's skin drained of color, which seemed impossible since he was already so pale. "Dominik said that he witnessed the Nightfall queen *consume* his power after it was taken from his body."

The room swayed as panic washed over me. "Lucien, what are you saying?"

"I'm saying..." Lucien leaned in even closer to me. "...that it appears the Nightfall queen now has Winter fae powers and whatever else she has... collected."

I didn't want to believe it. I wanted to ask him if this could somehow be bad information. But in the same moment, I also knew it was true. The Nightfall queen was hailed as an inventive genius. Her machines ranged from flying contraptions to mimic the dragons, to flame throwers and shooting projectiles. I even heard that she had created horseless carriages! This was entirely plausible, and it caused chills to run down my spine.

"What do we do?" I asked him.

He sighed, running a hand through his hair. "I think I need to go and speak to the other kings of Avalier. We should join forces with the others against Queen Zaphira."

I swallowed hard. "Go to war?"

It was everything Sheera and Marcelle had accused him of.

He opened his hands wide. "Do you see any other way? The Nightfall queen could have wind power, fire, ice! She could heal like an elf, spit fire like a dragon, and even have razor sharp claws like a wolf." His words were terrifying. "And if she can do this, what's to say her army can't? If we allow too much time to pass without action, we could soon be fighting a war not against humans but against... counterfeit magic users!"

He was right—as terrifying as it was, he was right. If we allowed the queen to bolster her army with these... magical infusions, we would soon be fighting a war we might not win.

"Do you think the other kings will join with us?" Together with the elves, the dragon-folk *and* the wolven, we would not fail.

Lucien sighed, looking tired. "I know they will."

"How can you be sure? Cockiness will get us nowhere," I chided.

"Because Raife came to see me with his new wife last week and asked if I would join him and the dragon king in a war against Zaphira."

My entire mood brightened. "Wonderful, what did you say?"

He pinched the bridge of his nose. "I said no and then punched him in the face."

"Lucien!" I scowled.

We might have only been in a courtship for less than a week but already I felt comfortable scolding him.

Lucien shrugged. "He bedded my... look, it doesn't matter. While you and I were in Spring Court, Raife returned with the dragon king, I presume to ask me again."

My whole body tightened. "And?"

"And my guards were instructed to bar them entry into the realm," he admitted.

I groaned. "This is not shaping up to sound like a good partnership."

Lucien grinned and I couldn't fathom what was funny about this.

"What is worth smiling about right now?"

A chuckle rose from the winter king's chest. "What I wouldn't give to have seen the look on Raife's and Drae's faces when they were turned away."

I smacked his chest and he caught my hand, pulling it to his lips to kiss.

"Do not worry." He held my gaze. "They are my oldest friends, and although we have had our trials, they will not deny my plea for help."

I raised one eyebrow. "So you'll ask for help?"

Lucien scoffed. "No. I'll wait until *they* ask,

pretend to think about it, and then join forces with them."

I grinned. That sounded like Lucien.

I knew the four princes of Avalier used to go on a yearly retreat when they were younger, something their parents set up to keep the magic races of the realm close. But rumor had it the retreats fell apart when the elf king's family was murdered by Queen Zaphira.

I sighed. "And so I guess this pushes our wedding further out." As a royal, you were never done sacrificing for your people. That was something I was about to learn the hard way. No one got married during a war. It was unsavory, spending money on a lavish wedding while men were dying in the fields. It would be at least a year now.

Lucien grasped the bottom of my chin and tilted my face up to look at him. "Go back to your home, gather your things and your family, and come back tomorrow. We will wed immediately. *Before* the declaration of war."

I gasped, my heart pounding in my chest as a lightness spread throughout my limbs. "But... tomorrow isn't enough time for a proper royal wedding. You're king and—"

"And I want my queen, not a seven-course meal and a cake taller than I am. Whatever my staff can put together will be fine with me. The Winter courtiers will be there as witnesses, and whoever else from your court you want to come. I don't need a big show. I just need *you*."

I just need you. Those words crept into my very heart and filled it until it was overflowing.

I prided myself on being able to conceal emotions well. Something I learned when training with my powers. Emotion and power were linked, so controlling emotions meant controlling power. But in this moment, I could not control the tear that slipped down my cheek, nor the gust of wind that rattled the window-pane outside.

It was the realization that Lucien loved me in a way I'd always dreamed of being loved. Without reservation. Without a care for what others thought, or reputation.

He reached out and swiped the tear from my cheek.

"I don't read women very well. Is this good crying or bad crying?" He looked down at me with concern.

I laughed, wanting to reach out and kiss him, but in a room full of people I couldn't. "Good tears. I'll see you tomorrow for our wedding."

It was early morning. If I rode fast now, and packed quickly, I could get back here with my family tomorrow afternoon.

There was a fire in his eyes now. "Until tomorrow." He pulled my hand to his lips again and kissed the top.

———

PIPER LEFT all of my things in my rooms at the Winter palace. There was no sense bringing them to Fall Court just to have to bring them back again. We rode fast on horseback knowing we would be lighter without the carriage. Lucien insisted on sending a soldier with me even though we were in my own realm, and I obliged in order to keep him happy.

The snow gave way to orange and yellow trees, and as we passed through the Fall Court village I waved to the workers at the market stalls. By the time we reached my house, I was sore and hungry but I didn't care. I was the most excited I'd ever been. Though a war loomed on the horizon, so did my happiness.

I jumped down from the horse and asked Piper and the soldier to put it in the barn for me. Then I ran for the small Fall Court palace that I had lived in all my life. I couldn't wait to tell my mother and father of the upcoming wedding. They would be a little shocked about the quickness of it, but, ultimately I hoped, happy for me. We all knew the Nightfall queen had been silent for too long, and now that we had evidence of her stealing fae powers and absorbing them I knew my father would agree with Lucien that we needed to join forces and strike quickly.

There was a strange carriage in the front yard with over half a dozen men who all wore gray traveling cloaks. My father often had visitors from the realm as he was the acting leader in these parts, and in charge of everything that happened here, but... these men gave me chills as I passed. They kept their faces hidden, and the carriage had a blanket over the door, covering the insignia.

Turning the handle to the front door, I slipped inside past a few of the palace staff and went right for my father's study.

I could hear murmured talking inside of it, two male voices, one my father's, and the other...

I yanked the door wide and snarled, "Marcelle."

The Summer prince spun wearing a deceitful grin. "Hello, darling."

My father jumped a little at the sight of me. "Madelynn, you're home."

The winds had changed in the room and he was doing the nervous tic he always did when he played cards, flaring his nostrils.

"What's going on? Why are you here, Marcelle?"

Marcelle's eyes glowered at me and the use of his name without title.

"*Prince* Marcelle..." My dad stood and stepped

away from his desk. "...is here to offer his hand in marriage so you don't have to marry that *monster* King Thorne, as you put it so aptly last week."

Hand in marriage? *What?* His words drew my eye to the contents of his desk. There was a small treasure chest like that you would use to pay a dowry standing on top of a signed document.

My heart hammered in my throat. "I'm already promised, Father. I just rode around the entire realm announcing my betrothal to King Thorne, who I am happy to report is *not* a monster."

Marcelle moved out of the way, behind me as my father approached me from the front.

"King Thorne has not paid the dowry yet," my father said, unable to meet my gaze. "So I am well within my rights to take another offer."

"Of course he hasn't, because you pay on the day of the wedding!" I shrieked, pulling wind from the cracked open window in my father's study.

Marcelle grasped my wrists from behind suddenly and then something pinched them, biting the skin. I gasped as a painful burning worked its way from my hands to my chest and the wind I'd pulled turned into stagnant, unmovable air. When I yanked my hands before me to see what he'd done, I whimpered.

"*Castration* cuffs? Marcelle, no." I pulled for my magic but was met with resistance and then nothing, as if reaching into an open void. "Daddy!" I screamed in panic.

A sob ripped from my throat. Castration cuffs were for those convicted of crimes. It inverted their magic so that they were rendered powerless.

My father stared at the Summer prince wide-eyed. "Marcelle, what the Hades are you doing cuffing my daughter like a criminal!?"

"She attacked me once before, only days ago. I could not afford it again. She's *very* powerful. I will take them off once she calms. You have my word." He used a syrupy sweet voice and I snapped out of my shock and fell to my knees before my father.

"No, please, Daddy. Don't do this. I love Lucien. There is war coming and siding with him is the only way!" I clung to his leg like I used to as a little girl when he would get home from a long week away.

Reaching down, he tipped my chin up to look him in the eyes. When I did, I was frightened beyond repair. He wasn't going to change his mind. I knew that look, that finality. "Marcelle has gone to the Nightfall queen and brokered a deal. She will leave Fall, Spring, and Summer Court out of the upcoming war if we separate from Winter and do not join the fight to come," he said. "I have to think of our people. Of your mother and sister."

I gasped, standing to my feet so fast that I nearly

knocked him over. "Traitor!" I screamed in his face. "Coward!" I yelled as tears streamed down my cheeks. "You've sold us to the queen! You've sold me to Marcelle!"

My father winced with each word and I was glad for it. I hoped it stung like Hades and he never slept again.

Marcelle's arm hooked under my armpit and he yanked me backwards. "I will keep her safe. She will want for nothing. She will be a cherished wife for as long as I live," he told my father.

Lies. The lies coming from his mouth were enough to drive me insane. I bucked against him but it only made his hold tighter. My father had checked out. He was just staring at the wall in defeat. I wanted to smack him in the face.

"Where is Mother?" I demanded. "She would never stand for this."

Marcelle pulled me from the doorway. "I arranged for your mother and sister to have tea in town while I spoke to your father. They are with my most trusted housemaid."

"Father, I beg you, do not accept this. I choose Lucien. He can pay double whatever Marcelle is asking."

My father sighed, again not meeting my eyes. "It's not about the money, Madelynn." His voice was broken and I didn't understand until Marcelle spoke: "Good man, you're doing what is right for your family and people."

I glanced up at Marcelle then, my mouth agape. "You told my father you wouldn't sign the deal with the Nightfall queen unless it included me as your wife."

Marcelle smiled then, a sickening smile that made my stomach roil. "You always were so smart."

My father was so afraid of war that he sold his own daughter to avoid it. Little did he know that war would come for him eventually. It would just be on a day not of his choosing.

"I forgive you, Daddy." It was the last thing I said to him before Marcelle dragged me out the door, then my father wailed like a little boy. I didn't want to leave him on bad terms. I hated him right now, but I also still loved him. He was hoodwinked and confused and he would regret this, I knew it.

As Marcelle marched me through my home, my brain was running a mile a minute. How could I get out of this? With my powers bound I couldn't fight. Could I talk my way out of it?

"This isn't legal," I told him calmly.

"It certainly is. Your father can negotiate many dowries, and only until it is paid is the deal done," Marcelle stated.

Was that true? I'd never bothered to read dowry paperwork. But it wasn't done like this. "Lucien and I have already paraded our courtship around the entire realm. The people will wonder—"

He cut me off. "The courts will be told King Thorne mistreated you. Not hard to believe. And then when the treaty with the Nightfall queen is announced, no one will care what King Thorne does. We won't be part of Thorngate anymore. He can do as he likes with his Winter soldiers and leave us out of it."

Panic rose up inside of me because the more he spoke, the more I realized that his plan was believable. Pulling my engagement ring from Lucien off my marriage finger, I slipped it into my pocket for safe-keeping without Marcelle noticing.

"The dowry is paid on the day of the wedding." That, I knew, was a legal rule.

He nodded. "And we will be married today. Right now in fact."

He yanked open my front door and then his men pulled back their hoods, showcasing the Summer Court insignia. The Winter Soldier Lucien had sent with me was unconscious on the ground, and I whimpered thinking of Piper, who was nowhere to be seen.

The blanket was ripped from the carriage and I was shoved inside.

"My things!" I shouted.

"Will be brought to you by my staff." He had an answer for every question. It drove me mad.

When I stepped into the carriage and saw a priest sitting next to a Summer courtier, my stomach dropped out.

Married now as in *now*. In a carriage?

Marcelle slipped into the carriage and pushed my shoulder down, forcing me to sit. He then looked at the priest and made a gesture indicating he get on with it. "Remember, Madelynn's father stipulated that I marry his daughter and keep her safe, otherwise he wouldn't join us in our separation," Marcelle told the priest.

"Lies!" I yelled.

Marcelle leaned in then, whispering in my ear. "Cooperate or I would hate for little Libby to have an accident."

My entire back went rigid, the fight going out of me in an instant. He had my mother and sister at the teahouse in town. He wouldn't hurt them, would he?

A tear slid down my cheek as I resigned myself to my fate. Nodding, I gave him a panicked look.

The priest began to read the wedding rites, and bile rose into my throat.

This isn't happening. This isn't happening. It was like my soul left my body. As we rode away from town, I nodded my agreement to the priest and relented to marrying Marcelle. When I looked out the window to say goodbye to my childhood home, I saw a flicker of hope.

Piper was running into the woods around the back of the house, towards the secret hunting trail that led to Winter Court.

10

I was numb the entire ride through the realm and into Summer Court. It all happened too fast. I couldn't process it. My powers had been bound, I was legally married to Marcelle, Thorngate was splitting, including Fall Court, and this would leave Lucien to fight the Nightfall queen by himself.

The thing that hurt most of all, the thing that I couldn't bear to think about, was my father's betrayal. The man who had kept me safe my entire life just sold me to the real monster. In his mind I was sure he thought he was doing right by me. This deal Marcelle had brokered with the Nightfall queen seemed great on the surface. Avoid an upcoming war, who wouldn't want that? But they were assuming she played by the rules, and I knew she didn't.

I just prayed that my mother and sister were unharmed and that Marcelle had only been testing me when he threatened them.

The thought of Lucien waiting for me to arrive and marry him tomorrow cut into my very soul and carved a mark on my heart. His mother died, his father was a lost cause, and now he didn't even have me.

We arrived at the Summer Court palace and I walked like a Necromere, devoid of life, through the castle gates with my head hung low as Marcelle led me to a room. The priest was still with us. Why the Hades hadn't he gone? We were married. He could—

Fear seized me in that moment and my head snapped up to Marcelle.

"Marcelle, I need time to adjust—"

He cut me off. "The marriage must be consummated to be legal."

I fully died inside then. Every bit of strength I once held as a powerful woman shriveled up and expired. Pulling for my power, I felt nothing. I felt for my rage but it was hollow. I was in shock. I was a shell of who I used to be. I must have blacked out, detached from what happened. There was a faint awareness of the priest confirming my purity, and then I barely felt it when Marcelle undressed me and lay me on the bed. He whispered into my ear that my mother and sister would be safe as long as I cooperated. There was a pinch of pain between my legs and then I got lost inside my head.

I remembered the day Lucien said that he saw me as he was passing by. I had been outside playing with Libby. She was practicing her wind power and was frustrated she couldn't make the leaves pick up off the ground and make a funnel like I could. So as she tried and tried and then started to cry, I told her to take a break. She needed to relax and just feel the wind. I made the leaves dance around us as we twirled carefree among the breeze. She laughed and threw her arms in the air as the leaves swirled around us. It was a happy day. I had so many happy days to focus on.

Like the night Lucien first kissed me. I hadn't expected to like him at all, let alone fall in love with him. But he'd crawled his way into my heart and now I was hungry for him, desperate at the thought that I would now never have him.

"Lucien," I whispered.

Marcelle froze on top of me and then there was a hard smack across my cheek. I instinctively pulled for the wind, and nothing happened.

It was in this moment, with Marcelle's quivering

body on top of me, that my shock dissipated. My rage came back to me and *I felt everything*.

The blood-curdling scream that ripped from my throat scared us both. Marcelle yanked himself off of me, rolling to the side, and I propped up on my elbows, reeling my fist back and connecting with his perfect, upturned nose.

"You bitch!" he growled, and then a bright blinding light went off before my eyes, stealing my sight.

"I hate you! I will never be your wife," I screamed, even though it wasn't true. I *was* his wife. I said yes and now he'd taken my purity.

It was done.

I blinked rapidly. *Whiteness.* That's all I saw. I yanked at the cuffs on my wrists but nothing happened except a searing pain. I was naked and screaming like a lunatic, when someone came up behind me and placed a cloak over my shoulders.

"Lock her in her room!" Marcelle yelled.

I felt like a feral animal who had just been caged. I reached out, blindly smacking whoever carried me and bucking in their arms.

"My lady, please calm down," a male guard's voice pleaded.

I couldn't see. I was powerless and I'd just consummated my marriage to Marcelle.

Rage didn't begin to cover how I felt.

I screamed, and thrashed against the giant guard who held me. I was naked with barely a cloak to cover me and I didn't care.

"Princess, stop!" the guard hissed.

I wasn't sure I could sleep at night if I didn't fight right now. If I didn't do everything possible to get out of here, I wasn't sure I could live with myself in the future.

But despite every fist I threw, and kick, it was no use. I'd never needed to physically fight before. I always had my wind magic. I was too weak.

The guard threw me onto a bed and slowly my vision began to return. Shadows moved around the room and then a door slammed, and a lock slid shut.

The full desperation of what had just happened weighed on me, and then with it a wave of shame. Why did I allow that to happen? Could I have fought earlier and stopped it? Would Marcelle hurt my mother or sister?

I was powerless.

I was married.

Not to Lucien.

Sobs wracked my body as I wailed into the blanket. Clutching for the pillow, I brought it to my mouth and screamed. I mourned the loss of something I had saved for Lucien. I'd wanted to experience that with him... and now I never would. I alternated between sobbing and screaming for nearly an hour until, finally, I passed out.

I WAS awoken to the sound of the hinges on the door squeaking. For a moment I forgot where I was, then the nightmare of my reality all came rushing back to me. My heartbeat spiked in my chest as I looked frantically at who was about to enter my room.

Please don't be Marcelle.

When I saw an unassuming handmaid, I relaxed a little. The door closed behind her and she bowed deeply to me. Her blond hair was tied into two braids and she didn't look a day over seventeen winters old. She wore the Summer fae crest on her brown apron, which she smoothed with her hands as she approached me.

"Hello, Princess Madelynn." Her voice was soft and calm. "My name is Birdie and I've been assigned as your lady-in-waiting."

"Birdie?" I didn't mean to say that out loud but it was a peculiar name.

She smiled, approaching the bed timidly. "My mother died in childbirth, so my father named me after her favorite thing—bird watching. I know it's not a common name, but I love it."

Her childlike innocence hurt my chest in that moment. Because it reminded me of myself a few days ago.

"I don't need a lady-in-waiting. I'm never leaving this room." I fell back into the bed and rolled over to give her my back. If I was going to be forced to bed Marcelle and then be locked up like a prisoner with my powers bound, then I wouldn't let him insult me with a lady-in-waiting like I was some honored guest of the palace or a real wife.

I could hear her swallow hard, and for a full moment she didn't say a word. I believed I'd stunned her and I felt badly if I hurt her feelings, but I couldn't play Marcelle's games and live with myself.

The bed dipped then, and suddenly she was hovering over me, her mouth to my ear. "The vote was held overnight. Summer, Spring, and Fall have separated from Winter. Marcelle is the new king of Hazeville, and once your coronation is held you will be our queen."

I wasn't sure I could be shocked any more until that very moment. A whimper lodged in my throat and I couldn't keep the sob from escaping. My father voted to leave Thorngate. Lucien just lost three courts... if the queen attacked... Winter would be overwhelmed.

Her hand rested on my arm and squeezed lightly. "I overheard King Marcelle talking to an advisor. He said he wants tabs kept on your mother and sister, that if you do not cooperate in this new role as his wife and queen... he will make them have an... *accident*."

I whipped around so fast that she jumped backwards.

"Why are you telling me this?" I looked at her skeptically, my mind racing as I thought up all the ways Marcelle could hurt my mother and sister. I shouldn't have fought back last night, it was stupid of me, but it wasn't in my nature to just lie down and take injustice with a smile.

She sighed. "I was serving in the dining hall the night you arrived with King Thorne. I was taken with his genuine apology, and I don't agree with how Marcelle has handled things. You were already promised to King Thorne and he just... it's clear you are here against your will and that doesn't sit right with me."

It seemed that against all odds, I had one ally in this place. I reached out and squeezed her hand. "Thank you."

She gave me a small smile. "Hopefully, I can make your time here as our queen more comfortable."

Time here as our queen. A lifetime. That's how long I would be here. I had married Marcelle Haze and it still hadn't set in.

How the Hades had all of this happened so

quickly? Did Lucien know yet? Surely word reached him about the separation. To know that three of your four territories had betrayed you would kill him, but not as much as me not showing up for our wedding.

A sob formed in my throat and I fell back into the pillow. A warm comforting hand was on my back then and I sniffled, pulling up from the pillow to look Birdie in the eyes. "Have you heard anything about King Thorne?"

She pursed her lips and shook her head. "Now that we've separated, no messengers are getting in or out of Winter. Fall and Spring have closed their borders and Winter is now considered... an enemy."

I gasped. "An enemy? The king who has kept us safe for years and we make him an enemy?"

Shame burned into her cheeks as she cast her face down. "No one wants war with the Nightfall queen. Marcelle made a deal—"

"I know about the deal." I sat up and looked down at my new lady-in-waiting. She was only a few years younger than me and yet seemed so much more naïve. "Do you really think Zaphira will spare us? The queen who has publicly declared her desire to wipe all magical creatures from Avalier?"

Birdie swallowed hard. "I suspect not."

"No. Marcelle bought you time. That's all. And in that time the Nightfall queen will grow stronger than

171

ever before," I growled. "Marcelle has doomed you all."

We didn't speak again after that. She went about tidying my new room quietly and then gave me a bath and brushed my hair.

I liked her, I did, but I wanted Piper. I wondered if my dearest friend had gone to Winter Court and told Lucien what happened. Did she even know what happened? Surely she'd seen Marcelle bring me out in cuffs and throw me into a carriage with the sun crest emblem. It wasn't that hard to speculate. I wondered if Lucien lashed out in anger that I'd taken another man, his rival, and then had sent her away. I wondered if possibly Piper would come for me here to at least live by my side as I walked through this new Hades of a life.

But no, the borders were closed as Birdie just said. No one would be getting to me. I felt the tears spring up again and bit them back. The time for crying was over. Now was time to plot my way out of here.

Three things I was sure of.

1. I loved Lucien Thorne. He would never forgive me for marrying Marcelle and giving him my purity, but I couldn't betray Lucien by playing queen to his enemy.

2. I had to get out of here and get my mother and sister into Winter Court, where I would beg Lucien to protect us. Even if I had to be stripped of my title and work as a handmaiden to whatever new wife he chose.

3. In order to accomplish all of this, I needed to kill Marcelle Haze.

With my newfound plan mapped out, I decided playing nice was the easiest way to get Marcelle to trust me again. Maybe he would even uncuff me and allow me to have my power back. Then I could use it to suck the air from his lungs until he turned blue and died. Something I now daydreamed of every moment.

My other idea was to smuggle a knife into my room, then request a night alone with him, to bed him. But he was stronger than me, and I was afraid he would wrestle the knife from my grip and then he'd never trust me again.

No, I had to play the long game and get him to uncuff me, releasing my power back.

Birdie left for a while, and when she came back she brought a whole handful of high-quality dresses. When I saw her putting them up in the closet, I was relieved that I could have my own room and not have to sleep next to Marcelle or... bed him every night.

"So I get my own room?" I asked her.

She smiled a bit naughtily at me. "I've informed Marcelle's head of staff that you have started your monthly bleeding and will therefore need your own room for the next week. It will give you some time to... adjust."

Relief washed over me at that. I had to bite the inside of my cheek just to keep from crying. She was truly what I needed in this moment, someone fighting for me when I couldn't fight for myself. I didn't need time to *adjust*, I needed time to plot Marcelle's murder. But I wouldn't tell her that. The fewer people who knew what I was up to, the better.

She'd just given me one week to earn Marcelle's trust enough to get him to take these cuffs off of me. Or for me to find a poison to place in his drink. I wasn't picky how he died, just that he needed to.

"Can you pick out a dress? I'd like to join my new husband for dinner," I told her.

She looked surprised at that but nodded. She dressed me in a light blue silk dress that I was horrified to find was custom made for me. Apparently the day my father had sent a messenger to announce my betrothal to Lucien, Marcelle had the palace seamstress prepare for my place as his wife. He'd planned this the entire time. Wasn't that the first thing he'd said to me when he'd seen me? That if he knew I was accepting proposals he would have given one to my father? He showed his cards right there and I didn't see it.

Now... how to make him think I wasn't faking my newfound compliance? Why would I want to have dinner with a man I'd just clawed at and punched the night before?

When I was dressed and Birdie had done my makeup and hair, I asked her to fetch Marcelle so that we could have a private chat before dinner. I was going to have to layer in some truth or he wouldn't fall for this new plan of mine.

When his knock came on my door a few minutes later, I crossed my arms and put on an angry scowl.

"Come in," I called sharply, and the door opened.

When he entered, he wore an almost identical expression. Mild irritation. But then his gaze drank in my hair, makeup, and dress and he softened a little. He shut the door behind him and the realization hit me that for the first time ever I was alone with a man in a room, without a chaperone, because he was my *husband*.

I swallowed hard. "You went about this all wrong!" I snapped at him. "You should have just told me you wanted to wed when I was here with Lucien. I had no idea your desire to become my husband. You blindsided me." My true anger was far more than I was displaying but he needed to see a little of it or he wouldn't believe my wanting to turn things around.

His brows knotted together. "And if I had told you, would you have accepted my proposal instead? I saw the way you defended Lucien. You cared for him. How he pulled that off, I have no idea."

I scoffed. "How the Hades do I know what I would have done? I was never given a choice. I *did* care for Lucien, yes. He was nice to me and I was under the impression I would be spending the rest of my life with him, so I stood up for him. Had I known *you* were a possibility, it might have changed things."

He pursed his lips as if he wasn't sure what to think about this turn of events. His brows lifted a little, dislodging their knot.

"I have been informed that the three territories have split from Thorngate and I am now to be queen of Hazeville, by your side, until the day we die," I declared.

He nodded curtly. "Yes." He looked proud. "I would like to arrange your coronation for tomorrow evening." Smug bastard, he had no idea of the damage he'd done.

I nodded, but in my heart I hated that I would become queen of Lucien's betrayal.

"Well then, we might as well try to repair the

damage you did in losing my trust, as I don't fancy hating my husband for the rest of my life," I told him.

He smirked a little. "I have to admit, hearing you call me your husband brings me great joy."

I was going to vomit, instead I just sighed and held up my cuffed hands. "After this, and your threats to my mother and sister, it will take a lot to bring *me* great joy."

Marcelle's face relaxed even more as if he was pleased with how this conversation was going. "Surely I have something to offer you that can bring you happiness?"

Take these cuffs off of me and leave my mother and sister alone! I wanted to scream. But that would show my hand too soon.

I chewed the side of my lip. "I hear Summer Court has the prettiest jewels in all the realm."

To even think I wanted diamonds at a time like this was insane, but he bought it.

"I will have my palace jeweler take you to the vault. Anything you like is yours."

I looked unimpressed. "Some chocolate cake wouldn't hurt either."

Marcelle reached for my hand and it took everything in me not to recoil. Pulling his lips to my knuckles, he kissed them. "Consider it done."

I nodded. "Alright then, I'll see you at dinner?"

"See you at dinner." He left with a smile and I hated myself for what I'd just done. But spitting in his face and getting thrown in a dungeon wasn't going to get me out of here. I was going to do whatever it took to survive this.

DINNER WAS BORING. It was just Marcelle and I. I was hoping for some courtiers, but no, Marcelle wanted to speak about all of his achievements and things he'd done since he'd seen me last at the Midsummer Festival when I was thirteen.

"I still remember what you wore that night," he said, and I tried not to react at the shudder that went down my spine. I had no idea he'd been pining for me this entire time.

"I remember your orange and cream outfit as well. The embroidered sunburst on the back was something," I told him. I *did* remember his outfit, because it was hideous and Piper and I spoke of it for two days.

Marcelle smiled at that, looking delighted.

This plan was working far better than I had hoped. I figured three more days and I would casually try to use my magic to lift something off the table, as if forgetting it didn't work, and let him see my disappointment.

Then he would offer to take off my cuffs. Until then, I had to play the part.

We were just tucking into the main course when one of Marcelle's Sun Guardsmen entered the room looking panicked. He strode quickly to the king's side.

"My Lord, I have delicate news." He looked to me.

Marcelle glanced at me also as if weighing things in his mind. I just rolled my eyes as if I didn't care either way and shoved a piece of bread in my mouth.

"Speak freely," Marcelle said.

"A cold is sweeping over the land." His news nearly made the bread lodge in my throat. "The winter king has learned of your marriage and his army rides to Spring Court, presumably to come this way."

I froze, unable to fake any sort of response.

Marcelle stared at me. "How taken with you was he? Would he freeze the realm again knowing you might also die?"

I didn't know what to say. "I honestly don't know what he would do. Now that I am married to you, he must have written me off and could freeze me to spite us both." It was an honest assessment, one I hated to admit I believed. He *could* do that. He would feel *so* betrayed.

Marcelle nodded and then looked to his guard. "Distribute the emergency stored firewood. Ordain a curfew. No one outside after dark. If the temperature plunges, we will be ready."

Emergency firewood? He had planned for this? Probably since the Great Freeze.

"Send the Sun Guard to Spring Court to join in their defenses. We can burn up the Winter Soldiers before they even set foot here." Marcelle grinned.

Burn them up. My heart hammered in my chest. If Lucien was busy fighting his own people, the Nightfall queen could choose this moment to attack and take down Winter Court. I just hoped she didn't get wind of it.

The guard ran off and then Marcelle turned to me. "His true colors are showing. After that whole speech about feeling sorry for the Great Freeze, he is about to make the same mistake."

It hit me then that Marcelle might have hoped this would happen. That Lucien would find out Marcelle had stolen his betrothed and that Lucien would react in a way that would further divide him against the people of Summer.

"Well, for our sakes, I hope not." I hugged my shoulders, wondering if I had imagined the sudden cool breeze that rushed into the room.

Marcelle reached out and grasped my hand, pulsing warm sunlight power into my arm. I wanted to yank my hand back but forced myself not to.

"You have nothing to fear at my side," he promised.

He had no clue. He really didn't know what Lucien was capable of. Could his Sun Guard burn Lucien's Winter Soldiers? In the daytime maybe. But if Marcelle thought he could win in a battle against Lucien himself, he was *sorely* mistaken.

The winter king could kill Marcelle from a hundred miles away, freezing the entire Summer palace and everyone in it.

So why didn't he?

A small part of my mind wondered if it was because Lucien didn't want to hurt me. He knew I was here and so he didn't want to freeze me too. But then why send a cold wave across the realm?

A chill rose on my arms because the temperature was definitely dropping. Was it a signal? To let me know he was coming?

I sighed. I could only dream of such a thing, but sometimes dreams were all we had to cling to.

Birdie had to come in twice in the night to stoke the fire in my room and add another log. It was cold, though not enough to kill. It was like Lucien wanted the entire realm to know he was angry that they'd left him and separated, and that he still had control over them whether they liked it or not.

I barely slept, tossing and turning, waiting for Lucien to arrive and save me—to march in and tell me he still wanted me and he didn't care if I was defiled and married to another man.

But he never came, and those thoughts weren't

realistic. So by morning I put on a heavy wool cloak and walked down to the dining hall. My door was no longer locked I was pleased to find, but the cuffs were still on, so I was definitely still a prisoner.

Marcelle was at the table already eating when I entered.

"Sorry it's late. I barely slept." I yawned for effect. As if not getting up early to eat with him truly bothered me.

He waved me off, looking annoyed. "Who can sleep with this chill? How that monster lives in the constant cold is beyond me."

I swallowed hard. Clearly Marcelle wasn't too happy with the weather either. "Can you warm things up? Bring out the sun?" I questioned.

Marcelle shot me a look. "Of course I can. But I don't want to deplete my power just so everyone can go outside and play."

Hmm interesting. I wasn't aware power depletion was an issue for him. I'd never run out of power. There was always wind around; air was everywhere. But when the sun went down or was hidden with clouds, it must render Marcelle weak. Did Lucien know that? Was that why he'd brought on the cold spell? Did he make the clouds roll in to cover the sun and weaken Marcelle?

"Understood." I sat down and began to butter a roll. "Any word on the Winter Soldiers at the border?"

Marcelle stared at me with slight suspicion and I rolled my eyes. "You can't tell me that my homelands are being attacked and not give me news! Fall and Spring are holding off Winter! Those are my people."

He relaxed a little. "The three courts fought Winter off all night and they retreated. They are no match for all three courts working together."

Just like the four courts working against the Night-fall queen would be no match, I wanted to say. He didn't want war and yet he'd still gotten one. How ironic.

"I've made an appointment for you to meet with the palace jeweler after breakfast. He's made a crown for your coronation and you can take whatever other jewels catch your eye. My mother had exquisite taste."

The mention of his late mother reminded me of his brother, Mateo. "Where is Mateo? I haven't seen him," I said, wondering if maybe they chose to live separately or he'd gotten married, though he would be quite young for that.

The corner of Marcelle's mouth ticked. "He was too rebellious, so I had to send him away for re-education."

Re-education. Too rebellious? It sounded like Marcelle had changed since I'd seen him at

Midsummer Festival all those years ago, and though I cried to my father for marrying me off to Lucien when I thought he was a monster... it was clear that the real monster was sitting right in front of me.

I FELT numb throughout the entire coronation. Fake smiles, false thank yous on the good wishes given to our union. It made me sick. With each passing moment I hated Marcelle more and more. I kept asking myself, how did I get here? It had gone too far and I'd played along too well to turn back now. I was stuck and constantly worrying about my mother and sister's well-being, so I didn't fight back. I stayed the course.

Get Marcelle to trust me enough to take these cuffs off, was my mantra.

I vowed in that moment to take sword training after I was free of here. I never wanted to feel so helpless again. Without my power I was weak. I hated to admit it but it was the truth.

As the crown was placed on my head and I took an oath to lead a people who had come against the man I loved, I died inside just a little bit. I had officially just become Lucien's enemy.

After taking as many blessings as I could handle, I then begged Marcelle to let me go for a walk.

"I'd like to see the townspeople and check out the shops. Make myself known to those who couldn't come today." Really, I just needed to get the Hades out of here. I wanted to be alone, to breathe the fresh air no matter how cold it was.

Everyone at the coronation was bundled up. Lucien's cold still plagued our land but it wasn't enough to hurt, just enough to not let you forget Lucien was mad about the separation.

Marcelle looked out at the thinning crowd as people made their way home, and then back at me.

I raised my cuffed hands. "I promise not to get into any trouble," I said sweetly.

He was quiet, and I hated that he had all the power.

"Am I really asking permission to go for a walk, Marcelle?" I growled then. "Am I your new wife and queen or a *prisoner*?"

I all but spat the last word and one of the guards turned in our direction.

Marcelle gave a nervous laugh and called two guards over to us.

When they stood at attention before him, he pointed to me. "Your new queen wants to go into town to be among her people. Please keep her safe and don't let her out of your sight." He then glanced at me. "Be good. Your mother and sister would be devastated if anything happened to you."

My face went slack at the veiled threat to my mother's and Libby's lives.

That bastard. That shit-eating, horse-faced, bootlicking bastard!

I pulled on my wind power and there was nothing and I wanted to scream, I wanted to punch Marcelle in his pretty face until blood dripped down his nose and into his mouth.

I realized then that there was raging murder inside of me. I had wondered, when the time came, if I were capable of killing a person, of killing him.

Now I knew.

I was.

I *would.*

This rotten excuse for a fae would suffer at my hand.

Greatly.

"Yes, darling," I said with as little venom as I could, and then turned on my heel.

Marcelle Haze would regret the day he took me as his wife.

THE FRESH AIR did wonders for my mood. It was chilly and I needed a thicker layer under my woolen cloak but the cold was nice. It reminded me of Lucien, and Winter Court, and snow falling on my eyelashes as I kissed him.

It felt surreal to still be daydreaming about kissing Lucien while I was now married to another man. I feared my mind was cracking as I struggled to cope with everything that had happened to me so suddenly.

The two guards that Marcelle had ordered to shadow me did in fact become shadows. They walked three feet behind me at all times while Birdie strolled beside me quietly. I liked her because she seemed to have the same knack for reading my mood as Piper did, and knew when to be silent.

People congratulated me and smiled and waved as I passed. Meanwhile, I wondered what they thought of the whole scenario. Just a few days ago they were waving at Lucien and I—albeit not smiling. Was that it? They were able to easily accept Marcelle stealing another's betrothed because they hated Lucien?

"I'm surprised they accepted this so quickly," I told Birdie, speaking for the first time on our walk.

Birdie looked at the women who wished me well and nodded. "Marcelle has made it clear he was sweet on you since you were young. Everyone thinks it's a love marriage and that you were being forced to marry Lucien."

I stopped walking and looked at her, again pulling for my wind power and again feeling nothing. The anger that boiled inside of me in that moment felt too raw to contain. It was as if I were made of fire and would burn up if I didn't release it.

Birdie must have noticed the shift in me because she looked alarmed. "Let's check out the local women's boutique," she suggested, and pointed to a store behind me.

I took three deep breaths, refusing to even process what she'd just said. I shoved it all down as a light snow began to fall from the sky.

The people gathered in the street pulled their cloaks higher and glared up at the sky as if cursing Lucien.

They had no idea. They had no idea that Marcelle had taken me against my will and that I was essentially a prisoner.

"The boutique has beautiful candles, perfume, knitted gloves..." Birdie trailed off, pulling me from my thoughts.

I nodded curtly, deciding it was better that I go into this shop and rid my mind of these murderous thoughts. Otherwise I would storm the castle with a blunt rock and attempt to beat Marcelle to death.

As we stepped up to the storefront, the guards moved to follow, and Birdie put out a hand to stop them before pointing to a sign on the door.

Ladies only.

"It's not proper. You must wait outside," she informed them.

It was a small victory, but I felt a tiny bit of joy leak into my desolate sadness as the guards stepped back and waited outside while we entered the shop alone.

Birdie was right, it was a lovely boutique. Candles that smelled like sandalwood and lavender, dainty gloves with flower embroidery. There was even a dressmaker in the back measuring a woman who stood on a pedestal in only her undergarments. Hence the no men rule.

Birdie was across the shop smelling candles, and I was just admiring an ornate glass brooch when the bell over the door chimed. Turning back to see who it was, I made eye contact with a young woman with black hair and fair skin. The hood of her cloak was up, dusted in snow, and she smiled at me.

She looked far too fair-skinned to be a Summer fae, but it did happen that the courts intermarried, so I assumed she was Winter fae or mixed. Turning back around to examine the brooch, I startled when she spoke to me.

"That's beautiful." Her voice came from right

behind me, and then I felt a tug on my cloak pocket. "Lovely weather we're having," she whispered in my ear, and then slipped past me and out of the shop as if she were a ghost.

My mind was trying to process what had just happened. I wondered if she'd just pickpocketed me. But I hadn't brought anything of value and her remark about the weather threw me.

It was horrid weather for someone who lived in Summer Court.

Unless she wasn't from here.

My heart beat wildly as I slowly slipped my hand into my pocket and felt a folded note inside.

Birdie looked over at me and held up a candle. "This smells like Summer Solstice!" she exclaimed happily.

I smiled, my mind racing with what the note might contain. Peering at the dressmaker and her client, I was pleased to see they hadn't noticed anything.

I didn't dare open it in here, there were too many eyes on me, the new queen. Walking briskly over to Birdie, I grabbed the Summer Solstice candle from her hand and put the brooch on top.

"I'll get it for you. Then I'd like to go back and lie down. Long day," I told her.

She grinned at the prospect of the free candle, and I paid for both items, charging them to Marcelle. I didn't want to look suspicious to the guards outside that we'd taken so long without purchasing anything.

Once we stepped back outside, my gaze darted around the market stalls and street shops looking for the woman, but she was gone.

Walking briskly, but not too fast, we made it back to the castle and I shut myself away in my room alone.

After pulling the letter from my pocket, I climbed into bed and unfolded it. When I recognized Piper's handwriting, a sob formed in my throat.

M,

I'm safe in Winter Court. We are trying to rescue you but all three courts fight against Winter! I am going to attempt to smuggle your sister and mother out of Fall because only I know about the secret underground tunnels. Stay strong. We won't rest until you are free.

-P

IT SAID SO much and yet so little. Was it wrong that my heart wanted a letter from Lucien? For him to be the one writing me? Piper said *we*. *We* are trying to rescue you. She and Lucien? She and his guards? Was Lucien doing it as a kindness, or... something else? At least he was granting Piper safety, and it sounded like he'd approved my mother and Libby to stay in Winter Court if extracted as well. Fall Court had two underground exit tunnels in times of war. They led out deep in the woods near the Winter border, so if Piper could get my mother and Libby out through those, it would be perfect. That was all good news... but... I ached to know what Lucien thought of Marcelle's and my forced union...

And yet I didn't need a letter. The snow falling from the sky, the crisp chill in the air, it told me everything.

He was mad as Hades.

I threw the letter into the roaring fire and then rolled over into bed. I never usually napped, I always had a lot of energy, but ever since I'd come here I wanted nothing but to sleep the day away and cry. I was trying to stay strong, to stay the course, but it was all starting to feel a little hopeless. And yet this letter gave me what I had needed to keep pushing on. So after prying myself out of bed, I went to have dinner with my husband and play the compromising wife.

I would get him to remove these cuffs, and then I would make his entire army watch as I stole the breath from his lungs.

If the people of Hazeville wanted a strong leader, they would get one.

Me.

12

At dinner, I droned on about how amazing the local shops were and the pretty brooch I'd gotten and was wearing. Marcelle smiled, complimenting the brooch and telling me how delighted he was that I loved Summer Court and was fitting into my role here.

We were just tucking into dessert when the temperature plummeted suddenly. The fire sputtered and Marcelle glanced at the servant with alarm.

The poor young boy added two more logs to the fire as he rubbed his hands together. I shivered, pulling my woolen cloak tighter around my shoulders.

Marcelle drummed his fingers along the table, looking at me. "I wonder, Madelynn, could you fight a cold freeze with your wind power? Push it back?"

Even mentioning such a thing, which would lead to taking off these cuffs, nearly made me weep with relief, but I had to play it calm.

I simply nodded. "Yes. I'm sure you heard that when Lucien lost control last time, my mother and I were able to protect my realm as best we could because of our wind power. We pushed the cold back somewhat. I was younger and my powers were not fully trained at that time. If he creates snow, I can push the flakes away from Summer Court and back to him. If he drops the temperature, I can move the clouds to expose the sun."

Marcelle nodded. "That's what I thought. *But* you could also peel the skin from my body, as you so aptly said before."

Hades. He remembered.

I popped a piece of chocolate in my mouth and acted nonchalant. "I could. Just as you could probably light me on fire. I guess you'll just need to trust me at some point, Marcelle. We are stuck together forever now."

He stared at me keenly but said nothing more on the matter. I hoped I was playing my slightly pissed but resigned-to-be-his-wife-forever role well. It felt like he was so close to letting me free and seeing me as an ally. If it got colder, if Marcelle thought the Great Freeze was coming back, surely he'd take off these cuffs and let me save everyone.

We ate the rest of the meal in silence and I prayed to the Maker that Marcelle was considering freeing me. Would I push the cold back to save his people? Absolutely. They were innocents in all of this. But not before I killed him first.

"I'm tired and cold. I think I'll retire to my room for the night," I told him.

"Goodnight," he said absentmindedly, watching the fire along the far wall and then looking at the frost covering the windows.

As I walked back to my room to withdraw for the night, I wondered if maybe I should hatch a backup plan. One where in the event that Marcelle never took off these cuffs, I could just flee this place. Being queen of the realm with bright red hair, I might be spotted, but with Birdie's help in buying food and paying for inns, I might be able to get as far as the Winter border. It was the riskier option, and involved me speaking to Birdie about my plan, so I decided to save it. If by day six of being here Marcelle had not freed me, I would flee or die trying. All I knew was I couldn't lay with him again. It wasn't right what he did and I'd never forget it. I'd never be able to *adjust* here.

THE REST of the night passed slowly, and the temperature dropped. It was hovering around freezing, causing all of the flowers in the realm to wilt and look ill. The clouds had completely blotted out the sun and it was pitch black. I barely slept, tossing and turning as the chill slapped at my face and my fire attendant added log after log, waking me with the sounds of crackling wood.

By morning, I was grumpy and overtired. When I walked with Birdie to breakfast, I noticed Marcelle was gone.

"Eat with me?" I asked her, motioning that she sit down at the table. It was set for two, with a platter of food in the center, and a roaring fire.

She nodded enthusiastically and took a seat next to me. I wanted to keep my relationship with Birdie strong in case I did have to flee and needed her help. I sensed her loyalty to Marcelle wasn't strong and she would stick by me, but I wasn't sure.

"Where is Marcelle?" I asked. She seemed to know a lot of the ins and outs around here.

"The king was gone at sun up. Something about the war at the border," she said.

The fact that Marcelle was now called a king bothered me greatly, but I was more focused on this war.

"Fighting each other." I clucked my tongue in disapproval. "My grandmother would be beside herself."

Birdie nodded, lowering her voice to a whisper even though we were alone. "My father thinks the fae should stick together. He voted against the separation."

I felt relief at that, and wondered if now was a good time to educate Birdie on my backup plan. Looking around again to make sure we were still alone in the dining room, I leaned forward and peered right into her eyes. "Birdie, you know that Marcelle took me from Fall Court against my will and force bedded me to make our marriage legal, right?"

Her cheeks reddened. "He said your father agreed and that he paid a dowry."

My fingers squeezed the fork I held as I tried to remain calm. "Technically yes, that is true. But he threatened to kill my mother and sister and paid the dowry to keep things legal." I held up my cuffed hands. "I am a prisoner, Birdie. You know that, right?"

She dipped her head in shame. "I suppose so. Yes," she finally admitted.

Good. I couldn't have anyone in denial right now.

"I need you to know that if by the end of my 'monthly bleeding,' I have not been freed from here, I will run away."

The words barely left my lips and her head bolted up, looking around frantically for listeners.

We were still alone. Doors closed. Fire roaring.

"But... Marcelle could find you." She looked terrified.

I nodded, grasping her hand and holding her gaze. "What I'm telling you is that I would rather die than stay here and play wife and queen to that monster."

She swallowed hard, and I watched the pulse in her neck sputter erratically.

She frowned. "Well, I don't want you to die."

That was good. I patted her hand. "Then when the time comes, if you assist in my breaking free from here, I will richly reward you."

I would force my father to pay her whatever she wanted.

She looked over at me then, studying my face. "Did you love him?" she asked suddenly.

I was confused by her question for a second, thinking she meant Marcelle, but her use of the past tense let me know who she was talking about.

Lucien.

"Yes. My father and I gave Lucien my word that I would marry him. And then Marcelle took that from me. Forever."

The finality of it killed me. Kings didn't marry defiled women. Nor divorced. Nor widows. Or even a woman with a scandal to their name. You must be perfect to be queen and I was not. Even if Lucien wanted to still be with me, he couldn't. It would tarnish his entire lineage and any children we had.

"That's not right. I'm so sorry," Birdie stated, and we ate the rest of our meal in silence.

I spent the afternoon rotating between walks in the garden with Birdie and reading in my room by the fire. It was positively frigid outside. A fine layer of snow had built up and wasn't melting off. I knew Lucien could kill the entire Summer Court by freezing us all to death and he was holding back.

I had to hope it was because he didn't want to hurt me.

THAT NIGHT, Marcelle was back from whatever frontline meeting he'd gone to. He had us served dinner right up next to the fire, but even so there was a chill in the air. It was as if Lucien's power had the ability to penetrate walls and was seeking the palace. Oh how I wished I had full use of my power. Even without an open window I could move the air around a room. That's usually what I used if I needed to break a window and then gain access to the unlimited air outside. I looked down at my cuffed wrists and frowned. Had I ever gone this long without using my power? We were encouraged growing up to use our power all the time because it helped us harness and control it. We would pass the salt at the dinner table with wind power or make paper flutter across the room. I was one of the most powerful fae alive and I'd been reduced to a dud.

Nothing.

I glared at Marcelle across the small table that had been set next to the fireplace as he tore into his stew like a slob. How he was raised a noble was beyond me. I hadn't asked him about war news and he didn't offer. I did not want to seem too eager to receive word about Lucien, but I was dying to know anything at all.

Marcelle's head started to move upward to gaze at me and so I dropped the glare and gave him what I hoped was an inquisitive look.

"Would you like to share the bed tonight?" he asked. "It will keep us both warmer." His eyes were hooded and I couldn't help the small tic of my muscles in reaction, but I prayed he didn't notice the visceral response my body was having to that question.

"I'm on my monthly." I grabbed my stomach, feigning embarrassment.

Thank the Maker for Birdie and her great idea.

He inclined his head. "I know. It would just be to share warmth. I promise."

No. No. No. Having him hold me all night long would drive me to insanity. I wanted to cut his manhood off for how crudely he'd taken my purity. My mother had told me that even in an arranged marriage the husband would be patient with the consummation, especially the first time. That it would be slightly awkward and might be over quickly but never rough or scary. Marcelle had scared me. He was too rough and what he'd done was *wrong*. I might not know a lot about lying with a man but I knew that. But I also needed out of here. I needed him to trust me enough to give me access to my power. Maybe this was how.

I had hesitated too long and now he was looking at me skeptically. I had to let a little bit of the truth leak into my answer or he would know I was lying. "You scared me with your eagerness when we... bedded. Excuse me for being nervous to be alone with you in bed. I'd never been with a man before, so I'm... shy and unsure how this part should unfold in a marriage."

His face lightened and he reached out to take my hand. "I'm sorry I was too eager. I thought you would try to back out of the agreement and I just wanted it done. I'll be slower next time and you'll enjoy it."

Unbridled rage built up inside of me then, mixed with nausea. He had no clue. I hated him. I wanted him dead. The thought of him touching me again made me grip the meat knife in my fist, but I forced myself to relax my fingers. "If it's just to keep each other warm, I think I would like that," I lied, trying to make my voice timid and not as murderous as I felt.

If he tried anything I wasn't comfortable with, I'd just have to resort to trying to strangle him and hope that I was stronger than him in that moment.

I let out a yawn. "I'm tired now. I'll retire to your room and you can join me later?"

I wanted to go in and pretend to sleep so that he couldn't attempt anything more than keeping the bed warm.

He nodded, his eyes glittering. "I look forward to it."

My heart hammered in my chest as I walked away from him. I was so angry at him, at myself for having to play this role. At my father. I was just so furious at everyone. Lucien would not have been forceful when we bedded. In fact, I knew he would not have pushed me to do it until I was ready. Grief welled up inside of me as I mourned a marriage and a lifetime that would never be. All the feelings I'd allowed myself to feel for the winter king had led to a deep love I didn't expect in such a short time. Seeing how his father mistreated him just endeared me to him more. I'd envisioned a life in Winter Court as his wife and queen, and now that dream was dead.

When I got to my room, I reached up and touched

my lips, remembering what it felt like to feel Lucien's warm tongue in my mouth. That kind of passion was unlike any I'd ever felt before and I suspected ever would again. Definitely not with Marcelle.

Birdie entered the room a short while later holding a white nightgown. "I've been informed you will be sharing a bed with the king tonight?" She gave a nervous laugh. It must be a shock after our earlier conversation.

My gaze cut to hers and the laughter died in her throat.

"I'm surviving," I told her.

Her lips pulled into a frown as she flicked her gaze to the floor. "Yes, my queen. I'm sorry."

I stepped closer, reaching out to grasp her chin until she was looking up at me. "Don't be sorry. Just know this about me: I will *never* be happily married to that man, no matter how much time I have to adjust."

Her frown deepened as she looked genuinely sad for me. I wanted to drill this point home with her because she might end up being my greatest chance at escape.

"Then I will do whatever it takes to help you get out of here," she said boldly, causing chills to race up my arms. "I was *not* raised to help keep prisoners. I am a lady-in-waiting to a queen and that means I put *your* best interests first."

My throat clogged with emotion. I didn't think she knew what it meant to me to have someone here that was on my side. "Thank you," I managed.

She glanced behind her as if making sure the door was shut and we were still alone. "Maybe if we can get you out of here, you could go to the winter king, ask if he would take you back. I'm sure Marcelle could find another wife. All of the ladies like him..."

I barked out a sarcastic laugh, shocking us both. "Birdie, the winter king will not take a divorcee who has already given her purity to someone else. I'm a royal, we live under a different set of rules than you do."

Her face fell and I hated that I was taking some of her innocence with this serious talk. She was clearly a hopeless romantic. "I just thought—"

"I'm damaged goods." I yanked the dressing gown from her and then shut myself away in the washroom. Once the door was closed, I fell against it and a sob ripped from my throat.

I'm damaged goods. I'd never spoken truer words and the gloom cut into me like a knife.

13

I debated asking Birdie to fetch me a knife from the kitchen and then hiding it under my dress. But if Marcelle found it, my whole plan was shot. I'd be thrown in the dungeon to never see the light of day. My wind power was my best chance of defeating him. Even in daylight, I felt that against his sun magic I would win.

After dressing in my nightclothes I made my way to Marcelle's room. Glancing at the bed where he'd so forcefully stripped me of my innocence, I swallowed hard and climbed in, facing the wall. The fire was crackling but there was frost on the walls and windows. It was getting colder. Lucien was still enacting his power from afar to show Marcelle that he was pissed.

It gave me comfort. Looking at the frost-covered window meant that even though Lucien couldn't have me anymore, he was decreeing some sort of justice for what was taken from us. It had only been a few days but I wondered if my elf contact had taken Lucien's father to the elvin treatment facility. I wondered if Lucien had contacted his friends, the dragon king and the elf king, to tell them of the news that the Nightfall queen was ingesting powers.

I wondered if Lucien's staff had prepared the palace for a wedding and then wondered why I never showed.

I hoped word had reached him that I had been taken to wed Marcelle against my will. It would kill me if he believed otherwise. I thought of the note from Piper that I had burned and prayed to the Maker with the tiny shred of faith I had left that my mother and sister got out. The second I eventually killed Marcelle, I would need to get my family to safety so that his men did not retaliate. I had no idea if they would still accept me as their queen once Marcelle was dead.

The door opened behind me and I pinched my eyes shut, evening out my breathing. Footsteps approached the bed, and then there was the sound of someone laying shoes and possibly a belt on the floor.

The bed dipped and my breath hitched slightly. Suddenly Marcelle's arms came around me and I mumbled something half intelligent, hoping to sound sleepy.

Don't touch me! I wanted to scream. His arm rested over my stomach as he tucked in behind me, his body flush against my back, and I decided that I *had* to end this tonight. It was now or never. I couldn't play wife to this monster and still respect myself in the morning. I would do a lot to survive, but my dignity had its limits.

Lying next to a man who'd robbed me of the chance to be with the one I *actually* loved, caused my mind to retreat to a dark place. I could feel my normally sunny outlook on life dying slowly as I imagined being stuck here forever.

No.

A plan formed in my mind as Marcelle's breathing evened out. I couldn't sleep if I tried, so I lay awake as the cool air filled the room and my cheeks stung from the icy air. Then I started to shake, chattering my teeth together for effect.

Marcelle roused behind me and sat up. He shivered as well; it *was* cold, just not as cold as I was making it out to be. Marcelle looked at the dying fire.

Standing from the bed, he walked over to the door

and wrenched it open. "Stoke the fire," he commanded a guard who was standing watch.

The guard entered and I kept my teeth chattering loudly. "Marcelle, please, let me push the cold back, at least for the palace. I'm freezing."

Marcelle stared at me skeptically. "We just need more firewood," he insisted.

Another guard rushed into the room. He was covered in a thin white frost from his hair to his toes. "My king. We've just had our first death, an old man, a farmer at the edge of our border. The freeze is starting there and heading this way."

Panic washed over Marcelle's face, and an equal measure of hope and dread filled me. Hope that Marcelle would free me and release these cuffs, and dread that Lucien had taken a life. I knew it would weigh on him and that he had little control over his power. He must be so mad at the courts for voting to separate the kingdom, and for Marcelle stealing me, that he'd finally lost control. Was his father there in the Winter palace saying awful things to him? I hoped to Hades not. It pained me not to be there to protect him.

I stood, throwing the covers off of me. "That's enough, Marcelle! No more lives need be taken. I'm the only one powerful enough to fight Lucien's frost."

Marcelle looked conflicted.

"My lord, children are crying in their homes," the

guard begged. "You can hear them as you walk through town. Something must be done."

Marcelle looked at my face and then the cuffs on my arms. After the longest ten seconds of my life, he peered back to his lead guard. "Bring me five of your most powerful men. I'm going to release Madelynn's power and I want protection in case she makes good on her promise to remove the skin from my bones."

Wow, he really wasn't letting that die. I wished I'd never said it. The thought of having *five* skilled Sun Guards aimed at me had *not* been in the plan.

I'd trained with my mother and father at the same time, throwing wind in multiple directions, but never to more than two people.

But it was the middle of the night, which meant they could not take from the sun and use their power indefinitely. They could only use their reserves, whatever they'd stored up the previous day. If I could cause them to use their power on me, but somehow protect myself, then when they depleted I could attack.

But how to protect yourself from fire when your power was wind? Wind fed fire, making it rage even bigger.

I needed Lucien.

I swallowed the whimper that tried to form in my throat and came to the conclusion that I would definitely be able to kill Marcelle, but then I would be overpowered by his guard and finally succumb. I didn't want to die, I wanted to live but I couldn't let Marcelle poison the realm with the separation and his deal with the Nightfall queen. It wasn't right. Taking him out would allow Lucien to take control again. My family and Piper would be safe.

There was a knock at the open door and Marcelle and I both glanced over to see Birdie. She appeared sleepy but held a thick cloak. "I overheard the guard. My lady should not be seen in her nightgown by anyone other than her husband." Birdie looked to the king. "It's not proper."

Bless her, she thought I cared about propriety in a time like this. I was just elated that I was going to be let out of these evil power-sucking cuffs.

He waved her in, an annoyed look on his face.

As Birdie approached me, she shook out the cloak, opening it so that I could see the inside lining fully. My brow furrowed when I realized she'd written something in charcoal across the cream silk lining inside.

The winter king is here, it read.

My eyes nearly fell out of my head, and luckily Marcelle wasn't looking at me in that moment, because I nearly fainted. Birdie hooked the cloak around my shoulders and buttoned it up around me, peering into my eyes to make sure I'd seen her message.

He's here? Like in the palace? How did she know?

Was he mad at me? So many questions ran through my mind but I couldn't speak any of them.

"My queen, will your power work best outside among the fresh air?" Birdie asked, giving me a look.

She didn't need to say anymore. Message received loud and clear. Lucien was outside the palace.

"Yes," I said quickly. "A cracked window is not enough to push the frozen air from the entirety of Summer Court."

Marcelle sighed, walking to his wardrobe and donning his own cloak. "Will this be quick?" he asked me.

I shrugged. "It depends on if the winter king fights me back."

Marcelle appeared unnerved by that idea but nodded. When the lead guard came back, I looked closely at the five guards he'd brought with him and was surprised to see that three of them were women.

It wasn't the fact that the women were powerful that surprised me, it was the fact that I might have to kill or injure one of them. In my mind, it was easier for me to kill a man. I didn't know what that said about me, but killing another woman didn't sit right with me.

I would try to knock them out, or blow them far away, but if it came down to it... I would do anything to be free of these cuffs and never go in them again.

I couldn't believe I was even thinking about killing

people. It had started with Marcelle, and now five other lives were about to be at my mercy.

Could I take the lives of these guards? I wondered as Marcelle led us out of the room and down the hallway.

I peered down at the cuffs on my wrists. The empty feeling inside of me was an ample reminder that I had no access to my magic, and I wasn't sure it was a feeling I could live with.

Yes, I told myself. If threatened with going back in these chains, I would kill to be free.

As we reached the door to the outside, Marcelle turned to Birdie. "You're no longer needed. Good-night," he told her, dismissing her.

She looked at me but betrayed nothing. She just dipped her chin once and then walked back down the hall to her room.

The winter king is here.

The words written on the inside of my cloak brought me trepidation and relief. Knowing that man's temper, I knew that if Lucien thought I left with Marcelle willingly or plotted against him, I might also meet my death tonight.

The frigid air greeted us as the doors were opened. Marcelle growled in annoyance.

The Sun Guard fanned out behind me as I stepped out onto the front steps overlooking the town square.

Every rooftop was coated in white and my breath was a puff of air before me. Snow fell from the sky in chunks and my skin stung as the pain of the freeze covered my body. It reminded me of that night all those years ago when I lost my grandmother. It was a bone-chilling cold that stung your very lungs as you inhaled. And yet this time my thoughts were not anger at the winter king, but compassion for him. To be afraid of your power, that it might unintentionally harm people, was something I'd never experienced.

I stopped in the open courtyard of the palace and held up my wrists as Marcelle looked me dead in the eyes. "I have an archer on the roof. If you harm me, he'll put an arrow through your neck." Then he leaned forward and planted an unwanted kiss on my lips.

I stiffened, my eyes going wide as they flicked to the rooftop to see an archer crouching with a bow aimed right at me.

Pure unbridled rage consumed me in that moment. Marcelle reached out, pressing his magic into the cuffs. Because he was the one who had closed them over my arms, only he could open them. There was a click and then he stepped away from me as they fell to the floor. The five Sun Guards fanned around me and I inhaled, pulling the wind into me.

Tears blurred my vision as I felt the well of my power open. I didn't realize until that very moment how much accessing my power completed me, how much it defined who I was.

One of the male Sun Guards stood right in front of me, hands held high as if ready to ignite my head into flames at any wrong turn.

"Move, unless you want to be blown into Spring Court," I growled, and he looked to Marcelle, who was at my back.

The guard must have gotten the permission he needed from the king, because he moved.

My mind was racing with all the possibilities. How could I take out Marcelle and avoid the archer until it was done? I knew I had to make it look like I was clearing the town of the freeze first so that they would relax.

With a simple exhale, I pushed at the air around me. It was everywhere, in my hair, under the eaves of the patio, inside my lungs. The fog that had rolled in and settled onto the ground moved as a giant gust of wind picked up and rolled through town at my bidding. The snow flurries moved with it, and the clouds, making way for warmer air. My hair lifted and was tossed around as a brilliant idea came to me.

"Marcelle!" I called over the wind.

He stepped forward, at my side.

"Have your guards channel their power into fire. I will push warm air through the town to melt the frost."

I didn't see his face, I was too focused on the task at hand, but he must have liked it because he barked for them to do it.

Now if only I could get them to deplete their power before I took out Marcelle. I might actually be able to make it out of this situation alive.

I could blow the archer off the roof to the ground below, but not without Marcelle seeing. My mind raced as the guards lit up their power one by one, calling fire into their palms.

I sent my wind weaving in and out of their hands lightly, collecting the heat and distributing it through the town. The windows and rooftops began to melt of their frost, and the temperature raised dramatically. The snow covering the ground turned to puddles, and a stream began to trickle in the draining ditches on the side of the road. It stopped snowing.

"It's working!" Marcelle sounded excited.

I felt no resistance to what I was doing, which told me that if the winter king was here, he was not fighting me. The freezing air and frosty mist were fleeing town easily.

A little too easily.

He's helping me.

Wherever Lucien was, he was... withdrawing his power to make it look like I was causing the temperature to rise so quickly.

Marcelle leaned into my side then, his lips brushing against my cheek. "You were worth every piece of gold," he purred.

And that's when I snapped. The caged, murderous animal inside of me that he'd created broke free.

I'd never tested the full capabilities of my power. I knew I could strip a tree of its bark in seconds, or an apple of its skin. I could toss a thousand-pound boulder from a mountain or snap a tree in half. I'd had to fight off my mother and father simultaneously in training as they attacked me from both sides. But I had no idea *just* how powerful I was until the moment Marcelle tested my patience and found it lacking.

Wind exploded out of me as if I were made of it. In that moment, it was like I no longer existed. I'd become wind and I was everywhere at once. My magic caressed everything in a twenty-foot radius, sensing where it was, and then exploded. The guards surrounding me went flying ten feet into the air, at the same time that Marcelle's body flew into the stone wall of the castle and then held there.

Because I was the wind and the wind was everywhere, I felt the moment the archer released the arrow. It hurtled through the air and I ripped it to splinters.

"Be reasonable!" Marcelle screamed as I stalked towards him, building the wind with me and creating a funnel in the courtyard. The wooden beams holding up the veranda creaked and the mortar between the stones crushed to sand. My feet lifted off the ground and I had to focus just to keep from flying away.

Reasonable? That bastard wanted me to reason with him after everything he'd put me through? It didn't even deserve a response. It deserved death.

I threw the wind funnel right into his pinned body and his screams of agony tore into the chilly night. For the first few seconds, hearing him in pain brought me joy, but then bits of his skin began to separate from his body and his screams turned to moans and pleas for mercy and my heart softened.

This was torture. This wasn't me. A clean quick kill was more humane. I could live with that.

My rage dissipated slightly. I pulled the wind back, but kept him suspended in midair, his arms and legs out like a star as his back rested against the cool gray stone. He was bleeding from a few spots on his face and arms. In his hands he held flickering flames as if he meant to attack me but didn't have the strength.

I stepped closer to him, holding his gaze with mine as I measured his breathing and the air intake in his lungs.

"Marcelle, you—"

The words hadn't finished leaving my mouth when a cold gust of wind hit my back and then over a dozen razor sharp icicles slammed into Marcelle's body. His neck, his chest, arms, legs and stomach were pierced simultaneously. He was pinned like a butterfly to a board. He barely uttered a wail when blood dribbled from his mouth and his head slumped forward, the sound dying in his throat.

He was dead.

I knew in that moment that Lucien Thorne was behind me, but I didn't have the courage to turn around and face him yet.

"Madelynn." Lucien's voice was a whisper, full of heartache and pain.

Tears threatened to obscure my vision and so I blinked them back rapidly, breathing in and out deeply.

I just stood there, frozen in shock and grief and *shame*. I knew that Lucien had just killed Marcelle so that I didn't have to, and now I was free.

"Sugar plum," Lucien tried.

It should have brought a smile to my lips, the fact that he was still showing some affection towards me, that he wasn't mad. But I didn't think he knew, he must not know the extent of it...

I turned finally, facing the winter king. He looked more handsome than I remembered, but my gaze went immediately to the giant black dragon standing behind him.

It was the dragon king.

Holy fae, he *flew* here with the dragon king? So that's how he got past the armies of three courts. He *flew*.

Shaking myself from my stupor, I lifted my head high as my bottom lip trembled and I caught Lucien's steely gaze. "Lucien, Marcelle and I were married in a carriage with a witness, and later..." My voice broke. "... that marriage was consummated against my will. It was all legal. So I'm sorry to inform you that I am no longer pure."

Anger flashed across Lucien's face and a blast of cold air slapped at my skin, causing the tears to fall to my cheeks and freeze there. Blades of ice shot from his palms and slammed into Marcelle's body behind me. I spun and noticed his crotch area was now pierced through with four ice shards.

As I suspected, he didn't know the extent of it.

Turning back to face Lucien, I closed my eyes, unable to see him like this, and then I heard him shuffle forward. His hands cupped my chin and then his lips were on mine. I gasped in shock and opened my eyes.

Pulling back from me, Lucien met my gaze. "Madelynn Windstrong, *everything* about you is pure. Your smile, your heart, your good intentions."

I was at a loss for words... "But the decrees state that a royal must be pure—"

"Do you think I'm pure?" he asked honestly, and I

blushed. The men were never really held accountable for that as there was no way to check. "I *never* wanted you for your purity, Madelynn, and tomorrow I'm going to change that decree."

That got a sliver of a smile out of me. "But I'm... married." My mind couldn't grasp what Lucien was saying, how he was acting.

Lucien pointed to Marcelle's dead body nailed to the wall with icicles. "Technically you're a widow now."

A sob escaped my throat. "Lucien, what are you saying? You still want me?"

I couldn't allow myself to hope. Lucien looked at me like I'd gone mad. "I didn't just convince my old friend here to fly me across the realm, while I froze everything in sight, so that we could be friends, Madelynn."

Laughter pealed out of me, then I rushed forward into his arms, peppering his face and collarbone with kisses. He wrapped his arms around me and just held me as I finally felt safe for the first time in days. I pulled back to look at him. "You're a good man, Lucien Thorne."

"Shh." He glanced over his shoulder as if checking to make sure no one was there. "I have a reputation to uphold."

The small flicker of hope that I had held since

Marcelle dragged me from my home roared to life. "I love you." I leaned in and kissed him again, my lips hungrily searching for his, not caring that it wasn't proper and that technically I should be a grieving widow who stayed single for a full year.

Forget the rules.

I was going to live for me and my happiness from now on.

Lucien eagerly returned my kiss and then pulled back and looked at the dragon king. "We should get going. The Nightfall queen has started a war on my border and she has an entire army of warriors with fae powers she stole from us."

I felt my eyes widen. "And you came for me? Are you crazy?"

He gave me a halfcocked smile. "A little bit."

So the stolen powers, she'd given them to her people! It didn't make sense, she hated magic. Or maybe she just hated that she didn't have any, and now that she did, she wanted to be the only one with it.

"What will happen to Summer Court? And Spring and Fall?" I asked, thinking of my parents and sister, and Birdie and all of the innocent people here.

Lucien gave me a look teeming with a mixture of rage and hurt. "*Hazeville* made their bed, they can lie it! Forget them. They're on their own." He spun to walk us to the dragon king and I pulled on his arm.

When he turned to face me, his gaze softened slightly.

"Darling," I cooed, and he steeled himself as if knowing I was about to ask something. "The people were just scared, and Marcelle may have forced them or forged some of the votes, we don't know."

Lucien shook his head. "It was not forged. The reason I had to fly here is because when I tried to come on horseback, I was fought. Fall, Spring, and Summer Guards *all* turned on me."

I frowned, knowing he was right, but thinking of Birdie and her father who were against the separation. An idea came to me then. "If the Nightfall queen sees that the fae are united again and Marcelle is dead, she might back off, which will buy you time to go and see King Moon." Axil Moon was the reclusive wolf king that I'd never met nor barely heard about, but I knew he was integral to Lucien's plan to join all the races against Zaphira.

The winter king sighed, looking dejected. "She has Summer and Fall power. Enough of it that she fought me off last night when I tried."

Shock settled over me which turned to anger. "She has wind power?"

"A lot of it, from multiple Fall fae I assume."

That thief! How many of our missing fae had really just been science experiments to her? Had she been taking them for months? I felt sick thinking about it.

The wind picked up behind me as I tried to calm my rage. "Marcelle is dead, which makes me the queen of Hazeville. I was coronated. I will gather my people and meet you at Winter Court. We will fight with you as one and then you and I will marry to solidify the merging of the fae back to Thorngate."

Lucien swallowed hard, his eyes glowing silver in the moonlight. "All I got from that was that you still wanted to marry me."

Laughter bubbled up from my chest as I reached out and raked my hands through his hair. "Of course I still want to marry you. But we have to put our people first and push back the Nightfall queen."

Lucien growled as if he didn't agree with putting the people first.

Out of the corner of my eye, I saw a troop of Sun Guards approaching.

Rushing forward, I kissed Lucien chastely and then pushed him towards the dragon king. "I will see you on the battlefield."

He frowned, not moving. "No, I won't leave you again."

I looked back at Marcelle's corpse. "I can take care of myself. I promise."

Surely he saw me fight off everyone. I'd only needed help with Marcelle because I didn't want to torture him. I'd gone soft, but I had intended to kill him.

Lucien hadn't left, and now the guards had reached us, pulling out bows and swords and igniting sun in their palms. Other Summer Court citizens were stepping out of their homes to see what the commotion was all about. When their gaze fell upon Marcelle's body they gasped and covered their mouths in shock. They stared from Marcelle's dead body to the winter king.

I threw a gust of wind at the guards and their swords and bows clattered to the ground. "Stand down!" I shouted. "Marcelle was lawfully executed for treason. I am your queen and leader now, and if you have a problem with that, then you may flee to Cinder Mountain," I told them harshly. We didn't have time for an uprising.

The dragon king chuffed from where he stood off to our left and I winced. "Sorry," I mumbled to him. Cinder Mountain was in his lands, but it was well known that's where everyone went when they weren't happy with their lot in life.

The guards looked around at each other, and then again at Marcelle skewered on the wall.

"The Nightfall queen is attacking Winter Court

right now," I told them. "We must unite against her or she will pick us off one by one!"

Not one guard moved. They all just glared with absolute hatred at Lucien. And he was glaring right back at them.

"Bow to your queen!" Lucien growled, advancing on them. "Or I'll freeze you all and be done with this entire charade."

The guards and people who surrounded us hesitated, stepping back a few paces and away from him, but then scrambled to their knees as a slap of cold air rushed at them. One by one, they kneeled.

Okay, I would have liked to have earned their loyalty, but fear worked too.

"Marcelle stole my betrothed against her will!" Lucien bellowed so that the amassing crowd could hear. "He tried to rob me of my future and he split our great land, which made us look weak. Now the Nightfall queen attacks, and if it were up to me I would leave you all to fend for yourselves."

We needed to work on his speech writing skills.

"But it's up to me, as your reigning queen..." I stepped up beside Lucien, hoping to calm his intense energy. "...and so I decree that if you travel with me to the Winter Court and fight as one, I will make sure you are well guarded against the war that is sure to come upon us. I will protect you as I would protect my own family."

The people looked nervously among themselves but remained silent, frozen in fear. No one wanted war, I understood that, but war had come to us.

The giant black dragon king flapped his wings anxiously.

"We have to go," Lucien said to me. "Come with me. If the other courts join us, then fine, but if not, I say let them live out their own mistakes later. I no longer care to protect them. They're ungrateful for the comfort and peace my reign brought to our lands."

Ouch. He didn't whisper that. As I was just deciding what to do, Birdie came out of nowhere. She jumped out from behind me and screamed, "Look out!" The warning had barely left her lips when an arrow lodged in my stomach. A burning pain like I'd never experienced before flared to life in my gut. It all happened so fast, it took me too long to register that I'd been gouged through with an arrow. My mouth popped open in shock, and then everything happened at once.

An agonizing scream thundered from Lucien's chest and icicles flung from his hands, piercing the archer atop the roof that had attacked me. The archer's body fell like a sack of flour to the ground.

Dead.

The people and surrounding guards gasped and began to back up in fear, whispers starting among them.

"No one move or I'll freeze you all!" Lucien bellowed and they stopped. "You *ungrateful*, vile people. How dare you try to kill her!" The sky let loose with a thunderous clap as clouds rolled in. His voice sounded on the verge of panic. The temperature plunged as clumps of snow fell from the sky.

Birdie ran to my side and caught me as I fell. It was weird. I knew that I might die from this and these might be my only moments left, and yet the only thing I could think about was the line of succession for Summer Court. We were still a split nation, and with Marcelle gone, and now me injured... "Birdie, you need to bring Prince Mateo back from wherever Marcelle sent him. He is in charge until I get back..."

The unsaid words passed between us as well. *He is in charge if I die.* She nodded, tears lining her eyes. Even in death, I was ever the perfect royal. My mother would be proud.

Lucien was there then, ripping me from Birdie's arms and tucking me to his chest. He grunted as he ran across the courtyard to where the dragon king waited. I peered over his shoulder to see every single soldier and townsperson on one knee, holding still for fear that Lucien would in fact freeze them to death. Lucien's eyes scanned the crowd as if ready at any moment to turn them into ice blocks.

I clung to him as he stepped into the basket that was tied to a saddle of sorts atop the dragon king.

"Are we seriously about to fly?" I muttered, trying to ignore the wetness and pain in my stomach.

Lucien kept his hand pressed to my wound, the arrow still stuck inside of me poking out between his fingers. "Yes, and it's rather fun in other circumstances."

With that, the dragon king's wings snapped out and he kicked off the ground, taking flight. A yelp of surprise ripped from my throat and then I coughed, wincing at a fresh wave of pain. I'd never felt pain quite like this. It was sharp and hot, and yet deep and throbbing as well.

"Shhh..." Lucien cradled me to his body, holding me so tightly that it hurt and felt good at the same time.

I looked up into his eyes and knew from the absolute terror marring his features that my wound was bad. A sudden sharp coldness pierced my stomach and I gasped, nearly passing out.

"I'm sorry, I had to freeze the wound. There's too much bleeding." He sounded like he was on the verge of losing it, and I felt bad for putting him through this. After losing his mom, and having a horrible father, I wanted to try to be a good thing in his life.

Blackness danced at the edges of my vision and I blinked rapidly to chase it away. I had no idea where he was flying me off to, what the point was.

"Lucien?" I whispered.

"Yes, sugar plum?" He leaned his forehead against mine.

Reaching up, I cradled his face and met his gaze head-on. I needed him to know something in case I went to be with the Maker. "I would have chosen you. Even if I had my pick of any man in the realm, I would choose you," I told him. Arranged marriages didn't give you the best confidence that you were wanted. I needed him to know that he was my choice, regardless of my father's input or our royal lineage and the rules set before us.

A whimper lodged in his throat and then everything became too cold. I couldn't tell if it was Lucien making it that way, or my soul finally going to be with my ancestors.

"Stay with me!" Lucien shook my shoulders and my eyelids snapped open. I fell asleep? When? I shivered, my teeth chattering as snow fell from the sky in clumps and thunder clapped around us.

"I'm sorry, my love. I have to keep you cold or you'll bleed to death," Lucien said, and then we made our descent.

"It doesn't hurt anymore," I told him through chattering teeth. "I don't feel any... th... ing."

He looked panicked at that, and the blackness at the edges of my vision grew wider until it encompassed everything. Suddenly I was drowning in blackness. My heavy body felt like it had fallen away and I was finally free.

LUCIEN

Madelynn's body went limp in my arms and my worst nightmare quickly became reality. Reaching up to her neck, I pressed my cold fingers there.

Nothing.

"She has no pulse!" I screamed to Drae, hoping my old friend could do something about it. His wings pumped harder as he cut through the Winter sky and then descended faster.

This isn't happening.

I looked down at Madelynn's face, studying every freckle and curve. It was as if on the day the Maker made Madelynn, he set out to create a masterpiece. Her face was carved of porcelain, smattered with freckles across her nose. Her sharp chin made her entire head resemble a heart, but my favorite thing was her orange and red hair, like bits of fire were trapped inside. The colors were different depending on the angle and if the sunlight was hitting it or not. I ran the pad of my thumb over her soft pink lips and what life I had stored up in my heart after my mother died perished in that moment. I was born a great lover of all things and people, but with every drunken rant my father beat the love out of me and turned it to hate and vengeance. The only person who'd kept it alive was my mother, and then she died and I was lost. When the teenage girl I loved had cheated on me with my best friend, Raife, my heart turned black and I covered it in steel, impenetrable to anyone.

Then I saw Madelynn dancing in the wind with her sister, the sun lighting up her hair like a roaring fire, and it was as if I'd been kicked in the chest. My heart flickered to life, dropping its steel cage and letting me know it still wanted to beat.

I had to have her.

I didn't blame Madelynn for hating me when she first saw me. I knew the rumors surrounding me were horrible—some of them even true. But when she stuck up for me with Marcelle and the Summer fae, and then again with my father, I fell in love with her so easily.

She owned my heart and soul.

I would do anything for this woman and now she was gone.

They always leave me.

I screamed into the sky as a frigid snowstorm blew around us. My powers were dangerous, and if not controlled would kill people, but I didn't care right now. My grief consumed me.

Drae dropped quickly, so quickly that I had to tuck Madelynn to my chest to keep her from flying out of the basket.

I failed her. Maybe I should have tried to find a healer in Summer, but would they have helped her? We just killed Marcelle and they didn't have any healer elves there, right? I was questioning everything now, every decision I ever made that led to this moment.

Suddenly Raife Lightstone, my oldest friend and the biggest pain in the ass, leapt into the basket atop Drae's back.

He was the greatest healer in all of Avalier. But he couldn't bring back the dead.

"She's gone." My voice was hollow, dead inside. My heart took its last beat and then began to stack an ice wall around it that I vowed to never thaw again.

I would never love another living soul, it only ended in disappointment. And they would never be her. Madelynn Windstrong could not be replaced.

Raife held his hand over Madelynn's face and his mouth popped open. "She's not gone yet. Her heartbeat is very weak but she lives," Raife told me, and grasped my fingers to squeeze them. He winced: "Brother, your fingers are too cold to feel her pulse. Calm this storm so I can get her inside!" he snapped at me.

Alive? I looked down at her: lips purple, chest not moving. Was he sure?

I couldn't see where we'd landed, the storm was raging too hard, a sea of white. I'd last left Raife at the Winter castle, so we must be somewhere near there.

Raife suddenly reached down and tried to wrestle Madelynn from my arms, and that got me moving.

"She's too cold. Calm the storm, brother. I need to get her by a fire." Raife shook my shoulders a little as if he were trying to shake sense into me.

"I had to freeze her to stop the blood," I told him mindlessly. I didn't want to allow myself to hope that she might still be alive. I felt like I was in a stupor. I'd gone into shock, I suspected, and I didn't know how to get out of it.

"Lucien, you're freezing her!" Raife yelled, and purple light exploded before me. His magic smacked whatever shock had its hold over me and it dissipated. It was like the storm clouds in my mind cleared instantly. "She's alive," he said again.

This time it hit me like an avalanche.

I dropped my power over the weather instantly. Standing, I clutched Madelynn to my chest and leapt out of the basket. My feet sank into snow that went up to my knees but I didn't have time to feel bad about hitting my town with the storm.

She's alive. She's alive. She's alive.

The last bits of snow fluttered to the ground.

Raife ran alongside me, his glowing purple hands hovering over Madelynn's wound as I ran inside the open entryway of my palace. My snow-covered boots slid on the cool stone floors as I fumbled to get her in front of the fire in the drawing room.

She was limp, her hair in half frozen chunks about her head and her lips purple. I feared that in my effort to keep the wound cold so she wouldn't bleed out... I'd frozen her to death.

Raife's strong hand clasped my shoulder and

squeezed. "You did good. She wouldn't have made it otherwise," he told me.

I backed away half a step as he knelt before the woman I hoped to one day very soon marry. Raife and Drae were once some of my closest friends but we'd grown apart. More than grew apart, Raife and I had a falling out due to his sleeping with the woman I loved at the time. I heard later that she'd slept with half my Royal Guard too, so he probably saved me from heartache, but that wasn't the point. The wound he'd inflicted so soon after my mother's death left a scar. I didn't think I could ever care for him again, or trust him.

Then Madelynn's lady-in-waiting arrived on bare horseback and told me what Marcelle had done. When she'd told me that he'd taken my betrothed against her will to have for himself, I nearly froze the entire realm just to spite him. And that's when Drae and Raife showed up. The second they heard the news about my future wife, they helped me fight my way to her at the border, and when that failed, Drae risked his life and flew me into Summer. I knew now that even though we'd had time and circumstances that drew us apart, I could always count on these men as brothers.

"How is she?" Drae's voice came from behind me and shook me a little.

Raife was hunched over Madelynn, throwing

purple arcs of healing light over her and grunting. He'd pulled the arrow out and it lay in two pieces beside her.

"Drae, I need you to fetch my wife. Fly as fast as you can. She's at the border with our armies making a show of togetherness for Zaphira. Tell her to bring her human medicine kit," he told Drae, and my stomach dropped.

I'd heard rumors that his new wife had an ability to bring the dead back to life. Was Raife afraid Madelynn would die? But her ability was not without great cost to herself, and I couldn't imagine him risking his own wife's life just to save Madelynn, no matter how good of friends we were. And a human medicine kit, how the Hades would that help us now? Raife was the greatest healer alive; no human concoction could touch his ability.

Drae bolted from the room, already shifting to his dragon form before he was even at the door.

"Talk to me." I didn't recognize my own voice. It was hollow and devoid of emotion, yet on the verge of panic at the same time.

When Raife glanced up at me, I didn't like the look in his eye. "I can heal any wound, shrink any growth, rid the body of nearly any poison..."

I didn't breathe, I didn't want to miss a word of what he was about to tell me. I wanted to be hit with the truth so that I could absorb it.

"...but I cannot make blood once it has left the body. I've closed her wound, but her heart... it's failing." He paused and a guttural wail ripped from my throat as the temperature inside the house plunged.

No. No. No. I couldn't lose her. Not like this.

Raife chewed his lip. "If Madelynn doesn't get blood soon, she'll die. My wife knows how to take blood from one person and give it to another to save them. I've seen her do it at our infirmary."

That sounded like Necromere sorcery. Something I wanted nothing to do with. "Put blood into her? Are you mad?"

He sighed. "I thought it was crazy too until I saw Kailani save a life doing it. My work is done, the wound is healed, but she *needs* blood."

Put an outsider's blood into her body? It was a wild idea that terrified me. But not more than the thought of losing her.

I looked down at her now ashen lips and went back to the memory of the time I first tasted them. I'd wanted to kiss her since the moment I laid eyes on her, and it did not disappoint. I wanted a thousand more kisses with her and I would not settle for less.

"Do whatever it takes," I told him, then I fell to my knees, cradling her head in my lap. "Give her mine," I begged him. "Please. Whatever she needs."

"Is her mother here?" Raife asked suddenly, peering around.

Her mother? So that she could say goodbye to her daughter? I leaned forward and kissed Madelynn's head. "No. I sent her lady-in-waiting to fetch her mother and sister before I kill her father for treason," I growled.

Raife cleared his throat as if he didn't like the idea of that. I didn't care. He sold her to someone else after she'd been promised to me. I would punish him.

"I was asking because it would be best to have someone she shares blood with. Do you have a staff member from Fall Court?"

My face fell, my stomach tightening into knots, and I looked up into my friend's eyes. "I do not hire staff outside of Winter Court."

That admission settled over us, and I didn't have the heart to ask him if Madelynn would die if we could not get Fall Court blood into her.

Just as I was wondering how long it would take one of my messengers to kidnap a Fall Court fae and bring them to me, Kailani arrived.

The half human, half elvin queen ran through my front door panting. She held a black satchel and her blond hair with a streak of brown in front was blown around her shoulders.

"I'm here. Talk to me," she said as she rushed

forward and opened the satchel, pulling out tubes and a needle.

"She was mortally injured," Raife told her as her gaze took in the dire position Madelynn was in. "Lucien froze the wound which saved her until she could reach me, but she lost a lot of blood. I have closed the opening but her heart is failing."

Kailani was wearing a pretty silk purple dress and yet she had no qualms about kneeling in the blood puddle at Madelynn's side and pressing two fingers to the side of her neck. "Do we have a next of kin nearby?" She hadn't looked at me yet, which was fine by me. She'd gone into healer mode and I'd rather she be focused on Madelynn. The last time I saw her I had hit on her and tried to kill Raife, so I would understand if she were even a little mad at me.

"No," Raife said. "And Lucien has no Fall Court staff."

Kailani put the needle into Madelynn's arm and then looked up at me. "I have no idea what this will do to her powers, but if you want her to live, give me your arm."

Her words shocked me. Her powers might be affected? Did I care about that right now? *No.* But she might. Still, if she were alive to yell at me for messing up her powers, I didn't care. I would pay all of the gold in my vault to be yelled at by her again.

Without question, I extended my arm and Raife placed a hand on his wife's lower back. "Are you sure this will not harm Lucien's power?"

She shrugged. "The average body has more than enough blood to spare. He will grow his back while he sleeps. He might be weak in power for a day or two, but that's it... I think."

Weak? I'd never been weak in my life. I hated to even think of it. But Madelynn was worth it.

"Just save her. Please," I begged. I would grovel if needed, but Kailani didn't require it. She simply wiped a wet cotton ball across my arm and then poked a needle into it.

I flinched, not really at the pain but at the sight of my red lifeblood leaving my body and filling the tube she'd connected to it. It streamed down to where Madelynn lay on the floor and went into her arm.

"This is wild. Are you sure this will work?" I'd never seen something like this before in my life, and I'd seen a lot of healings growing up.

Kailani nodded. "We don't have healers in Nightfall where I grew up. Humans have to use other things like inventions and medicines to survive. This is one of them. When a person loses too much blood, it can be donated from another person." She looked worried, her face hiding something.

"Then why do you look so concerned?" I asked her.

She chewed at her lip. "We don't know why yet but some people have reactions to blood donations."

I stiffened. "What kind of reactions?"

She took a shaky breath. "I've never heard of someone dying but... in Madelynn's case it wouldn't be good since she's already so weak."

All the hope I'd had for her to make it out of this was quashed in that moment.

"Maybe I can help if there is a reaction," Raife offered.

Kailani gave him a sweet smile but she didn't look too confident.

"That's why you asked about her mother or someone from Fall Court?" I said.

Kailani dipped her chin in agreement. "Next of kin is always the best. Blood closest to hers is less likely to have a reaction."

My heart began to hammer in my chest and I wasn't sure if it was because I was now low on blood or if I was just processing her words.

"Have you ever done this on fae?" I asked her.

She shook her head. "Humans and elves only."

Great. "So you have no idea what a Winter fae giving blood to a Fall fae will do?"

Kailani swallowed loudly, her mouth thinning to a line. "I do not, but I know that either way you've bought her time. If your blood fails, we will know pretty quickly, and by then the mother and sister should be here."

I held on to that, on to the promise that even if I couldn't save her, maybe I'd bought her time so that her mother could.

A few minutes passed as I stared at the pulse in her throat. Was it my imagination or did it look stronger? Kailani was mumbling under her breath, counting. I assumed timing how much blood I could lose before I myself needed a donation.

After what seemed like forever, Kailani pinched the tube and then pulled the needle out of my arm and did the same to Madelynn. She then threw the tube and needles into the fire and looked up at me. "How do you feel?"

Panicked. Heartbroken. Desperate.

"Fine," I mumbled.

Raife scanned his hand over Madelynn's chest, then her stomach, and grinned. "Her heartbeat is stronger. I don't sense any reaction yet."

Yet.

"When will she wake up?" I took her cold hand into mine and realized that the house was freezing. I was horrible at keeping my emotions in check, and since my power and emotions were tied together, it made things difficult.

"She just needs rest," was all Raife said.

"Let's get her in a warm bed. I'll change her into some dry clothes," Kailani offered.

Her clothes were wet from snow and blood and so I nodded. I knew she'd rather her lady-in-waiting change her, but she needed to warm up and rest, so I allowed it.

After carrying her to her room upstairs, I sat her on the bed, holding her head up on my shoulder as I looked away from her.

Kailani made quick work of stripping her clothing and throwing it on the floor. I continued to hold her head against my chest as her limp arms were flopped around by the grunting elvin queen, until finally Kailani told me I could look.

Madelynn had been changed into a simple white dressing gown which looked dry and warm. I set her head back on the pillow and tugged the thick woolen blanket up to her chest. Then I pulled a chair up to the side of the bed.

Grasping Madelynn's hands between mine, I rested my head on the blanket and tried not to lose hope.

"Do you need me to stay as a chaperone until her

lady-in-waiting shows?" Kailani asked from the open doorway.

The fae were very proper in our culture about purity and marriage. It was why I was going to go back the first chance I got and cut Marcelle's manhood from his dead corpse for forcing himself on my future wife. The very thought made me want to freeze the entire Summer Court realm. I looked down at Madelynn's sleeping face and the soft rise and fall of her chest. We weren't officially married yet, I had not bedded her, and yet she already felt like my wife.

She was my forever.

"I think we're past that," I told Kailani, "But you can send in my head maid to be sure." I didn't know what Madelynn would want. Her reputation was important to her and I didn't want to tarnish it any more than it had been.

Kailani nodded and then moved to leave.

"Kailani," I called out after her.

She turned to look at me in the doorway with a soft expression, and I couldn't help but feel that my friend Raife had struck gold with her. She'd just rode on a dragon's back at a moment's notice to save Madelynn after the way I treated her and her husband the last time I saw them.

"Thank you," I said.

She smiled and gave me a slight bow, which was gracious of her considering she was a queen herself.

A few moments later my head maid arrived. She took the dirty dress from the floor and tossed it out before setting up a chair in the corner to read.

The hours passed. Raife came and went, checking on her and telling me everything looked good. My lead guard gave me news on the warfront. The Nightfall queen had been quiet since I'd stopped the storm. We both agreed she was probably using the moment to regroup and bolster her defenses. I just didn't care right now.

The stress of the last twenty-four hours weighed on me. It had been a ruthless nonstop war with my own people to get Madelynn back. Not to mention this attack from Zaphira at my border. I was exhausted. And so I gave in to the pull of sleep with my face on the blanket beside Madelynn's stomach. I never cared much for belief in the Maker. After losing my mother and then being constantly abused by my father, I couldn't fathom a Maker that would allow that. But my last thought before I fell asleep was a prayer to the Maker that he would let Madelynn live and make her my wife forever.

Madelynn

Awareness pulled at my mind and my eyelids snapped open. I took in the ceiling above me in confusion and then everything came flooding back. Lucien killed Marcelle, then I was shot. I was flying on the dragon king and then it got so cold... I passed out.

Lucien.

I realized then that a heavy, slightly cold hand was

laced with mine. I gazed down into the sleeping face of the winter king.

I smiled at the peaceful look he carried, something he rarely did. Peering around the room, I noticed a slumped figure in the chair in the corner. One of Lucien's maids. She must be a chaperone. I found it sweet that he was still trying to protect my reputation even after everything that happened with Marcelle.

I wiggled a little to adjust myself and Lucien's head shot up into the air as he looked at me wide-eyed.

"You're alive," he breathed.

I smiled, reaching out to touch the worried lines around his eyes. "I am, thanks to you."

If he hadn't frozen my wound, I'd have bled out right there in Summer Court.

Lucien didn't move, he just stared at me in shock as if he didn't believe this moment was real.

Without wasting a second more, I leaned forward and pulled his lips to mine. I no longer cared about propriety or purity. I wanted Lucien's lips on mine as many times a day as possible. He whimpered into my mouth as we hungrily tasted each other. Yesterday, I was pretty sure I was going to die, so I wasn't going to waste another moment of my life not living it to the fullest.

He pulled back abruptly, shaking his head and looking stricken. "Wait, Madelynn, you don't understand. Raife couldn't save you, not fully. His wife had to do a special procedure."

"Procedure?" I cocked my head to the side and he leaned his forehead against mine.

"You lost too much blood... so they gave you mine."

His confession horrified me. *Blood?* "Gave me yours?" I asked, confused.

Lucien cleared his throat. "They placed my blood inside of you."

They put his blood *inside* of me? I shivered at the thought. It sounded like dark sorcery, which I was wholly against. But I was happy to hear I hadn't ingested it.

"Lucien, how? Necromancy?" Only the vile monsters that lived in Necromere did blood magic, or so I'd heard. They kept to themselves. I hadn't heard of or seen someone from there my entire life.

"It was a human contraption. Not dark magic. I made sure," he tried to reassure me, but I was still panicked at the thought.

Lucien's blood was inside *my* body?

It was in this moment that I looked down to see what I was wearing. When I noticed my dress had changed, my eyes bugged.

"Queen Kailani changed you. I didn't see anything," he assured me. Would it even matter anymore? I'd nearly died. Lucien seeing me naked before marriage was the least of my concerns.

"Are you okay?" I asked him, checking his body for signs of injury.

He showed me his arm and the tiny red dot where they must have taken the blood. "I'm fine but... I confess I don't know what this will do to your magic or your body. I'm sorry, I had to make a choice and—"

I put a finger to his lips to stop his frightened rambling. "I would give up all of my magic if it meant I could live a long life with you."

A stomach-dropping grin graced his face and he gazed at me with adoration. "Marry me. Right now."

I chuckled at that. The morning light was just filtering into the room and I reached up to touch his face. "I would love to marry you. Is my family on their way? Piper's note said she was getting them out."

His face changed then, a mask of anger for a split second, but long enough for me to notice. I realized my mistake then.

I'd said *family,* which included my father. A man who'd betrayed him.

Although I knew in my heart Lucien could not allow such a betrayal to go unchecked for fear of looking weak, I also loved my father. I hated him for what he did, but loved him for who he was my entire life.

"I meant my mother and sister. As far as my father is concerned, strip him of his title if you must, but please don't kill him," I begged, reaching for his hand.

"I have every right to take his life," he growled.

He did. But I knew he wouldn't. He was hot tempered, but when he stopped to think it through he wouldn't cause me one ounce of pain. I knew it.

"My mother can lead Fall Court, and she will side with Winter. He did everything behind her back," I told him. "She and my sister were innocent."

His steel gray eyes looked deeply into mine. "Maker help me, I can deny you nothing."

I smiled, relieved my father would keep his life. After his betrayal, my father would not be welcome here, and although it saddened me I wasn't ready to see him either. I needed time and space before that wound healed.

"Come, let's get breakfast and prepare to wed the second your mother and sister get here," Lucien said. "The Nightfall queen has retreated for now."

That was welcome news. The ladies' maid helped me bathe and dress, and I met Lucien in the large dining room.

The second I walked in I was reminded of his father and our altercation here.

"Oh, Lucien, I forgot to ask about your father. Did the elvin healers come for him?"

Lucien looked down at his plate and a sadness fell over his face. "They did. But at the last minute my father chose the other option you gave him. He's currently enjoying endless mead and wine in a cabin in the mountains."

My heart plunged into my stomach at his declaration. After all that, he chose to stay sick. I walked over and ran my fingers through Lucien's thick dark hair. "I'm sorry," I told him.

He looked up at me with an unwavering strength. "Don't be. It's the first time I've felt at peace in my own home since my mom was here. I was always afraid to ask him to leave for fear of the fight it would cause between us and what my power would do."

My chest tightened at his declaration and I allowed him to pull me into his arms. It was bittersweet. Nice that his dad wasn't here to hurt him and bully him any longer, yet sad that he wasn't willing to get help.

"Maybe when we have children he'll change his mind and want to—" My words were cut off when the door to the dining hall burst open and slammed against the brick wall.

My mother stood there with Piper. Both looked stricken with pale faces and snow-blown hair. My mother's cheek was bleeding from a small cut and Piper was covered in dirt and leaves.

I scanned the space behind them, a stone sinking in my gut. "Where is Libby?"

My mother swayed on her feet. "The Nightfall queen's men tried to take her. But I fought. She's okay."

I leapt forward just in time to catch her as she fainted.

Lucien burst from the table and came around to help me lower my mother to the ground as Piper kneeled before us, cradling her arm to her chest. She was injured.

"Talk to me, Piper!" I barked. She seemed to be in shock.

"Your dad and mom fought them but... they had fae powers. Wind, snow, fire, uprooting trees." She paused and I steeled myself.

"Where is she, Piper?" I rested my mother's head lightly on the ground and stood, ready to ride to their location and get my sister back.

"She's here. In your room with a nurse. She's shaken but fine," Piper told me, and looked at me head-on. I could see the trauma hiding behind her eyes. My friend would never be the same after what she'd seen. "Maddie, they had metal *wings*. They tried to *fly* Libby out of there. Your mother..." She stared down at my mom's limp form. "I've never seen her like that. She was *so* powerful, she flattened every tree for a mile, but... she depleted her power saving Libby."

"No," I sobbed.

My sweet mother. Depleting your power as a fae could be a permanent thing. You used up so much of your magic in one moment that the well ran dry.

"Are you sure?" I asked.

The room was suddenly plunged into a deep coldness. I looked up at Lucien. His eyes were practically glowing silver. "The war has begun. This is inexcusable."

I rushed towards him as my mother started to moan and awaken. Piper bent to help her while I placed my hands on Lucien's chest. "Please. Please, tell me we're going to get revenge for this. She went too far," I growled.

A conflicted look crossed his face and my stomach tightened.

"Of course we will, Madelynn, but we can't rush out right this second. We need to rally an army."

I was afraid he would say that.

My throat pinched with emotion as I tried to remain calm. I wanted to suck the wind into the room and throw it at a tree, but I had to keep my head. "If we wait too long, Zaphira might take someone else important." How dare she try to kidnap my sister! Was she going to drain her of her power? The very thought made my blood boil.

"I could plunge her entire lands into a death freeze,

257

but I'd risk killing the innocents there," he told me. Therein lay the true issue. We knew from reports of defectors that had fled the Nightfall realm that innocents were there who hated Zaphira, and they didn't deserve to die for the actions of their mad queen.

There was a knock at the door and I looked over to see a beautiful woman with white hair that held a brown streak in front. She wore a regal dress and stood next to a dapper-looking elf. I knew instinctively this was the elf king and queen.

"We heard about the attempted kidnapping. How can we help?" the queen said.

I nearly cried in relief.

"Zaphira is getting bolder. We must strike a blow so that she knows this was unacceptable," Lucien told the elf king.

Raife Lightstone nodded, his moonlight-colored hair shaking around his shoulders. "I've been waiting years for this war, you know that."

I was so grateful to have these men working together to ensure nothing like this ever happened again. The thought of my mother or sister being taken filled me with so much fear I felt sick.

"I hate to ask this..." I looked to the elf king. "...but my lady-in-waiting is hurt." I motioned to Piper, who held her arm to her chest as my mother lay in her lap.

Without a word, he knelt next to Piper and waved

a glowing purple hand over her arm. Her face, which was previously pinched in pain, relaxed, then he went to work on my mother.

"She just needs rest. Exhaustion." He peered up at me from my mother, who was in and out of consciousness.

"Thank you," I told him. "And thank you for helping heal me." I looked to the elvin queen. "Both of you."

She smiled at me as the elf king waved me off like it was no big deal. I suppose he saved lives every day and it wasn't a big deal to him. But it was to me.

"Do you have spare healers you could send to the battlefield when we strike?" Lucien asked the elf king, completely going into war mode, which I appreciated. The fact that the Nightfall queen had gone after my sister left me feeling angry but also afraid. I'd mistakenly thought we'd have a few months until we were in full-blown war, but the war had begun like Lucien said. There was no way we could let Zaphira get away with trying to kidnap a royal and live. We needed to crush her before she did something even more bold.

"Absolutely. I'll ready them now," the elf king declared. The elvin people were known for their healing. Even the weakest among them had some sort of healing power, and they were all expert archers. Having them in battle with us would be priceless.

"We have the Winter Soldiers," Lucien told me, "Every single one of them will do as I ask."

I stared at my mother. She seemed to have gained her composure, and stood with Piper's help. "Fall Court is already suiting up and heading this way," she told me. "Your father stepped down in leadership this morning and left me in charge."

There was shame in her voice. I knew she must be so disappointed with how he'd handled things. Their marriage was strong, and I hoped it would survive this. Lucien hadn't yet stripped him of his title, but he would when he had a moment to breathe. It would devastate my father, who had served our people for decades, but he'd made a mistake selling me to Marcelle and backing out of the agreement with Lucien. If he kept his life, I considered us lucky.

"If the Nightfall queen has Summer and Spring Court powers, then we will need them too. I will go rally the remaining courts," I declared.

Lucien growled. "They *left* Thorngate. Let them go! Zaphira will come for them eventually and I will deny their pleas for help."

I snapped my head to glare at him. "I am their queen now, Lucien! So they will do as I say, or may the Maker have mercy on their souls."

Lucien looked impressed at my outburst. Maybe it

was the tone in my voice but I believed he knew I would not return here without an army.

"So what's the plan?" I asked.

Someone deeper down the hall cleared their throat and we all turned. It was hard to miss the dragon-folk, they were built like horses and this one was no different. The man before me, who I assumed was the dragon king, as I'd never seen him in human form, was a massive gentleman, as tall as Lucien, and as wide as two Luciens. He was stacked with muscle, his black hair braided into a ponytail at the back, similar to how Lucien wore it.

He stepped into the dining room, my mother and everyone moving out of the way so that he could do so, and then bowed lightly to me. "Good to see you doing better, my lady. I'm Drae Valdren, the dragon king."

"Madelynn Windstrong," I told him, and curtsied.

"So, I admit I was eavesdropping, and I have a plan on how to retaliate on the attempted kidnapping of your sister," he declared. "It will win us an edge in the war and buy us time to get Axil Moon here."

I didn't care that he had been listening in and only wanted to hear about his plan. King Drae Valdren was a force to contend with. He once flew into Nightfall territory to kill Queen Zaphira's son as retribution for murdering one of his people. If he was talking, I was listening.

Drae clapped Lucien on the back. "The winter king will build up a ten-foot wall of snow and ice at the border. This will buy time for Raife to get his healers in here."

Lucien nodded. "I can do that easily."

Drae then looked at me. "This also buys you and I time. I will fly you back to your people and you will convince them to join the war."

I tipped my head high. It was a great plan. "Let's leave at once!"

Drae chuckled at my eagerness. "I've sent for my wife. By the time she gets here, you and I should have returned, with backup on the way. While the fae army attacks at the border, it will draw Zaphira's forces out."

Lucien grinned. "And you fly over them and rain fire."

Drae nodded. "Arwen can fly too. We can reduce their numbers considerably."

"The Nightfall people have magic powers now," I said. "What if you are both killed?"

Drae rubbed his chin in deep thought. "She's got a point." He then peered at Lucien. "If we die, freeze everything and avenge us."

Good night! That was morbid.

Lucien chuckled. "You know I would."

Kailani cleared her throat. "As a last resort, right? Because there are good people in Nightfall, people who hate Zaphira and just want to leave. She keeps them under curfew and forces them to join the army at a young age."

We let that settle over the room. It was easy to want to wipe out an entire people over the actions of their leader, but it didn't make it right.

"As a last resort, yes. Until then, I will rally the rest of our people and we will show Queen Zaphira she's messed with the wrong fae," I growled.

Lucien cleared his throat. "No offense, sugar plum, but we aren't sure your powers are still working. I'd hate to send you off alone without knowing you can protect yourself."

I'd completely forgotten about the blood. Just the thought of Lucien's blood running through my body made me feel a little queasy. But there was no time to dwell on that.

"Then let's see if my power is still intact, shall we?" I said to the room.

My mother had stayed quiet nearly this entire time, but now she was frowning. "What happened to your power?"

A few of us chuckled and I led everyone outside, explaining to my mom on the way what had happened with the blood donation. We all walked through the back garden area to a small open field. There was a thin sheet of snow on everything and it was *cold*. The trees had no leaves and it was the perfect place to practice.

Lucien, the dragon king, the elf king and queen, my mom, and Piper, were looking at me.

"No pressure," I laughed nervously.

"I'm just glad you're alive. Whether or not you are powerful anymore doesn't matter," Lucien said.

It was sweet, really, but I would be devastated. One thing I'd always felt confident about was my wind magic.

Dropping my fingers to my side, I splayed them out. The group behind me stepped back a pace and I called the wind to me. It whistled through the trees' frozen branches, causing the icicles to break off and fall to the ground. It was a warm up, and good so far. Opening my eyes, I reached out my right hand and allowed a fraction of the rage I had built up for Queen Zaphira leak out of me and embolden my power. A wall of wind ripped through the canyon to the right and slammed into the tree, breaking it in half. There were gasps behind me but I stayed focused on my power.

There was something new there, something wild and cold and reckless. I pulled on it, letting the magic flow out of me, and yelped when an ice shard flew from my palm and slammed into the trunk of a tree.

I dropped my hold over my powers and then spun,

facing Lucien with wide eyes. My heart rattled against my chest like a bird in a cage and I feared he would somehow be mad.

"You have some of *my* power." He sounded in awe.

"That was amazing!" Kailani added.

The elf king rubbed the back of his neck. "Well, now we know the blood donation worked. It more than worked."

That made me beam. "Do you think it's permanent?" I asked.

The elf king peered at his wife, who shrugged. "No way to know. We are on new ground with this. But I'll take extensive notes in my medical journal and leave a copy with you in case you ever need to use it with your people again," she said.

I gave her a smile of gratitude, but I was worried about what Lucien was thinking, and everyone seemed to catch on to that because one by one they left to go back inside.

"Are you mad?" I asked him, stepping closer so that he could pull me into his arms.

He did, wrapping them around me tightly. "Never. I'm surprised and happy. The more powerful you are, the more protected you will be," he said.

I frowned. "Then why do you look sad?" I asked. Maybe he didn't realize how much he wore his emotions out in the open, but I could tell by the look on his face that something was bothering him.

He shook his head. "Nothing. It's selfish."

I peered up at him, craning my neck. "Tell me!"

He planted a kiss on my lips and then pulled on my hand. "I'll show you."

We walked past the snow-covered garden and to a giant cathedral I hadn't noticed in the distance. It was made of stone and stood two stories high, with dark wooden arches and ornate trusses. As we neared, I gasped at the beautiful stained glass depicting the phases of the moon, along with all of the different elements.

"I didn't know you had a cathedral in Winter Court." Cathedrals were usually associated with those who worshiped the Maker. We had many in Fall Court. But Winter Court was rumored to be lacking in the belief of a higher power or a preordained destiny.

"My mother had it built. She demanded to my father that she had a place to worship the Maker," he said as he reached for the ornate engraved wooden door. I smiled at the thought of his mother demanding his non-believing father build her a cathedral.

When he opened the door, I stepped inside and a little gasp of surprise escaped me.

There were hundreds of white flowers, freshly

hung from the ceiling, lining the aisle and all over the front altar. No one knew what the Maker looked like but we knew all came from him and all returned to him, so we envisioned him a lot like the bright shining sun that hung in the sky. *Giver of life.* A huge orange and yellow sun was centered in the far wall of the stained glass. It cast buttery hues along the white flowers.

"I'm sad because I wanted to marry you here. *Today.* I didn't want to wait, I didn't want to have to fight Zaphira right now. I want to live out my life in peace as your husband."

I spun, blinking away tears, knowing that these flowers were fresh because he'd asked his staff to ready this room to marry me.

I sniffled. "When did you have this done?"

I wanted to be selfish too. I wanted to marry and not have to rush off into dangerous territory and possibly get killed.

"Yesterday, before I left with Drae to come get you. I told my staff I was returning with my bride to be and we would marry at once. Then Zaphira attacked and you got hurt and... well, you know the rest." His face looked downcast.

"I'm sorry." I grasped the sides of his jaw. "I promise you, after I get Spring and Summer to send their troops to the war, we *will* marry. I'll go now and be right back. With Drae flying, I can be back in a few hours."

He sighed, looking upset. "Last time you said that, you were taken by another man and I found you half dead."

I pulled him to me, crushing his lips against mine as an ache built in my core. Did he have any idea how much I wanted him? I'd never desired anything more in my life.

Pulling back, I held his gaze. "I *will* marry you, Lucien Thorne. I swear it on the Maker in this house of worship."

Lucien grinned. "Now you have to or you'll be struck by lightning."

I laughed at the old wives' tale. "Exactly. So have no fear."

Lucien reached up to thread his fingers through my hair and pulled my face to his lips, planting a kiss on my forehead.

The door to the back of the cathedral burst open and a guard rushed in. It was in that moment that I realized I had been alone with Lucien, without a chaperone, for the first time and I didn't care.

The guard was wearing the emblem of a messenger, and he was wheezing from running too hard. Before he could open his mouth to speak, the ground shook, causing a crack to splinter one of the artistically designed glass windows of the cathedral.

I gasped, looking at Lucien.

"What was that?" he bellowed.

The messenger spoke then. "Queen Zaphira is at the border with a thousand men. We need you."

A thousand! *Already?* She was mobilizing quickly.

"She's going to try and take out Winter because she knows of the separation," I said.

Lucien took in a deep breath as if to calm himself. "Then go and rally your people. If a single one of them hurts you again, in *any way*, I will freeze Spring and Summer, taking the life of everybody there. I don't care how many innocents die."

His declaration sent chills down my spine, mostly because I knew he would. There was a darkness inside of the man I loved, one I constantly had to keep in check.

There was a very real chance that I would die trying to bring Summer and Spring soldiers back here. They'd already tried to assassinate me once. This would rob Lucien and I of the future we so desperately wanted with each other. So as I stood in the courtyard, looking up at the man I loved, I didn't know what to say.

Leaning into my neck, Lucien planted a kiss there and then moved his lips to my ear. "You brought me back to life, Madelynn," he whispered against me, and my entire body ached.

You brought me back to life.

His words reverberated around my head and I took comfort in knowing that at the very least, if I died, I had mended his heart for another. Let the woman who came after me love him greater than I did, because he deserved it.

I took two steps towards the black dragon waiting for me and then thought better of it.

If this was possibly my last time seeing Lucien Thorne, I was going to make it count.

Spinning, I ran for him. The heat in his eyes matched the heat buzzing around my body. I leapt into his arms as they came around me, tightly crushing me to his body as our lips found each other with a hungry need. We weren't married. We didn't have a chaperone. Our tongues were dancing together in full view of the public and I didn't care about any of it. I needed to taste him before I left.

When his hand came around the back of my hair and tugged gently, I whimpered into his open mouth and he swallowed the sound.

We finally parted, both panting, and I ached for more. Standing on my tiptoes, I pressed my lips against his ear. "My heart is yours, Lucien Thorne. Now and always." With that, I pulled away and spun around before I could see his face. I didn't want to cry. I didn't want to go into this as an emotional wreck. I needed to be strong.

I hopped into the basket with Piper, who sat beside me, and the dragon king took off into the skies. I tried to focus on the task ahead and not about the war or what Lucien was doing right now. I knew he was more than capable of protecting himself and his people. He was the most powerful fae among us. But the Nightfall queen had been stealing our magic for months! Not only did she have a thousand warriors at our border, she had them... *enhanced*, with our power.

Now I had to do my part. We couldn't ask Archmere and Embergate to fight beside us when we ourselves were broken. I had to unite Thorngate once more. It was going to be a large group effort to get everything assembled in time to fight Nightfall back and push them off Winter's border.

I reached out to grasp Piper's hand. She was being quiet, and I knew she was probably in shock. I told her she didn't have to come but she'd insisted. I'd barely been able to check on my mother and Libby as I'd run out of the Winter Court palace. Both had been asleep, an elvin healer with them. But Piper, my loyal friend to the end, was waiting for me with Drae.

"I never got to say thank you for the letter. It gave me hope and kept me going!" I yelled over the wind.

Piper peered over at me then, tears brewing in her eyes. "I'm sorry I didn't stop the carriage. I should have thrown a rock or—"

I cut her off. "What? What are you talking about?"

Her voice broke. "When Marcelle took you, I saw the whole thing and I didn't know what to do. I'm not powerful like you are. I knew I couldn't fight, so I ran to get help, but now I wonder if I had tried to fight—"

I pulled her into my arms and she fell into sobs, shaking against my chest as she exhaled her pent-up grief. Was this why she'd been so quiet? She felt guilty for not being able to save me?

"Piper, they would have killed you. You did the right thing. The best thing. You told Lucien so that he could save me." I stroked her back as she cried. I felt bad for not realizing she'd been carrying this guilt.

"Did he...?" she muffled into my jacket. "...did he hurt you?" She pulled back and looked into my eyes. I knew what she was asking: did he *bed* me? Piper took guarding my purity very seriously, and I knew this would kill her. She had to know.

"The marriage was legal," I told her, trying to avoid saying anything that would be too graphic for her. "But Lucien still wants me, so it doesn't matter."

It did matter. A small part of me died that day and would never come back. That innocent, carefree childhood part of me that thought the world was a safe place and I would always be protected was dead. But Piper didn't need to know that.

She looked beside herself. "I'm... I'm so sorry."

I grasped her shoulders and forced her to look at me. "It's not your fault. Nothing you could have done would have changed my fate."

She frowned. "I hate being so weak in my magic. I want to learn swordsmanship!" she suddenly declared.

I grinned. "I was thinking the same thing when my magic was bound. Let's learn together."

She nodded, and then snuggled into my side.

The rest of the ride was smooth and took no time at all before the peaks of the Spring palace came into view.

"Land there!" I yelled over the wind to the dragon king. I'd been managing the wind for optimal flying speed for him, but I was still coming to terms with my ability to call snow and ice into being. I wondered if it would be permanent or last just a few days. Kailani had said it was experimental in nature so she wasn't sure. Either my blood would absorb and flush his out, or bind to it, keeping his magic with mine forever.

Either way, it was kind of cool to have. It felt so much more volatile than my fall magic. Winter was volatile in nature and so it made sense. I had a little more compassion for Lucien now and how he'd handled all these years with this power.

People began to come out of their homes, looking up and pointing at the dragon streaking across the sky.

"There's Sheera!" Piper announced, and then glanced over at me. "Do you have a plan?"

I sighed, watching my friend step out into the garden of her home and look up at me. I didn't want to do this the hard way. I wanted to be soft and loving, but Sheera and her parents had plotted an uprising against my future husband behind my back. Did they also know Marcelle planned to take me for himself?

No. I couldn't think that they would and not warn me.

Still, niceness had only gotten me so far in life. It was time to fully embrace this queen of Hazeville title I now carried.

Sheera's mother, father, and household staff were in the garden, as well as half a dozen courtiers and a handful of guards. The dragon king landed expertly before them and I jumped out of the basket attached to his back, landing on my worn leather boots.

"Madelynn?" Sheera grasped her chest in shock at what she was seeing. No doubt she'd never seen a dragon, as I had not before yesterday.

"You may now address me as Your Highness. Or did you not hear? I was married to Marcelle and I am now your queen." I tilted my chin high and carried every ounce of royal superiority I could.

The air instantly changed. Sheera's eyes went wide

and she gave me a light curtsy. "Of course, Your Highness. I heard."

I felt bad for causing my old friend to speak to me
in such formal terms, but I could make no mistakes
here. Any friendly banter might get me taken advantage of, and time was of the essence.

I glared at her parents, the real perpetrators in all
of this. "You made me your queen and now you will
live with *my* rule," I growled. "Zaphira tried to kidnap
my sister—" they all gasped, even some of the courtiers
"—and the winter king is currently holding her off at
the border while I bring reinforcements. So gather your
army and head to Winter Court or I will kill you for
treason and failure to follow orders."

Duke Barrett's mouth hung open like a gasping
fish. Then he laughed. "My darling, you may be my
queen in theory, but I take *orders* from King Marcelle."

He didn't know. Word hadn't reached him. I
grabbed the wind around him and raised his body up
into the air.

Sheera and her mother shrieked, backing up and
looking at me wide-eyed.

"Marcelle is dead! And you will be too if you do
not make it very clear where your loyalties lie," I
bellowed. "The Nightfall queen is coming for all of us!
The treaty Marcelle made with her was never taken
seriously. She still encroached on Fall Court lands and

tried to kidnap Libby. She only wanted to divide our people! You will either unite and help us or you will be ripped apart by this wind!" The leaves and dirt spun in a small whirlwind at his feet as I held him above the air. I knew he had great power over the dirt in the earth and the rain in the sky and could probably swallow me whole, but not before I took the breath from his lungs.

He seemed to be considering it too.

Sheera's mom jumped in front of her husband. "We are with you! Madelynn, look at me!" she commanded. I'd known this family since I was a little girl. The way she said my name reminded me of when I was small.

I looked at her and found there was compassion in her gaze. "It was a mistake to split the realm. To think that the Nightfall queen would leave us untouched. We were just trying to protect our loved ones. But it was a mistake, and we are with you. Right, Barrett?" She looked up at her husband.

He sighed, the wind swirling around him and causing his hair to fly across his face. "We're with you," he said, resigned.

I dropped the wind holding him and he fell to his feet.

"The dragon-folk, the elvin people, *they* are with us too. This is the right thing to do. Unite against Zaphira as one," I told them.

Everyone on the lawns' gazes then went to the very large dragon behind me, and to Piper who stood next to him. As if in agreement, he huffed out a smoke-filled breath and stomped one large scaly foot.

"And for the record, the winter king is a good man that I love and will marry," I added. They looked less on board with that but I didn't care. "Take your army and ride to Winter. I will bring up the rear with Summer Court."

Sheera looked at me wide-eyed. "You killed Marcelle and yet you think Summer Court will follow you?"

Technically, *I* didn't kill Marcelle, but I wasn't going to go into that right now. "They had better," was all I said before walking over to Drae and mounting the saddle basket on his back with Piper.

Barrett began to bark orders at his men to ready for war, then the dragon king kicked off the ground.

One court down, one to go. There was no time to waste.

"I wanna be you when I grow up," Piper said, and snuggled into my side. I laughed then, so grateful to have her to lean on in these uncertain times.

We sat back deeper into the saddle and shared some dried meats and fruit. I could barely eat at a time like this but I needed to keep my strength up for the battle ahead. King Valdren was an extremely fast and capable flyer. I could be back in Winter Court and ready to help with the war within a few hours.

I just prayed to the Maker that Summer Court would be easy to convince, because whether they liked it or not, we were at war.

WHEN WE REACHED SUMMER, I was relieved to see a large gathering in front of Summer palace. People were filing into the meeting hall off to the side of the main structure. King Valdren landed in the same garden where I had first kissed Lucien, but this time when I dismounted he began to shift into his human form. I turned away, giving him privacy as I knew that his shifting did not involve keeping his clothing. I took the fact that he was changing into his human form as a sign that he wanted to accompany me on this one, so I waited patiently as he slipped into the guest house and came back out wearing clothes that were four inches too short at the wrists and ankles.

"I have a bad feeling about this one, and I promised Lucien I'd keep you safe," he told me. Walking over to the saddle that he had crawled out of, he reached into a bag and hefted his sword.

It was very chivalrous that he thought he could

protect me, so I did not take this time to educate him that I could steal the very breath from his lungs.

"Thank you," I said and we walked together, with Piper, towards the meeting hall where murmurs and shouts could be heard all the way from here.

I looked at King Valdren and he nodded. It seemed his assessment of this place was right. Their leader was dead. Last they'd seen of me, I'd been shot with an arrow, and now I was going to storm in and force them all to go to war.

Maker, give me strength.

The crowd was so large that we slipped into the back of the meeting hall unnoticed.

"We should march on Winter Court and burn the king alive!" someone screamed.

Chills raced up my arms at the mention of such treason. I peered onto the raised stage to see a lone man, a boy, really, no more than sixteen winters old. He stood erect, listening to his people as they shouted what they thought he ought to do.

Prince Mateo.

Marcelle was always jealous of his little brother. It was rumored that he was so powerful he could light a man on fire with his mind, so Marcelle apparently had him locked away, for *re-education*.

I was glad to see that Birdie was able to get him from wherever he'd been.

"Quiet down!" Mateo shouted at his people. But they just got louder. I could see the panic in his gaze. He might have had royal blood, he might be powerful, but he was not a born leader, nor had anyone given him training.

"Permission to toss you on stage?" King Valdren whispered into my ear.

Perfect.

"Granted," I told him.

Next thing I knew, the dragon king's giant hands grasped my hips and he picked me up, carrying me over three rows of people, and deposited me on stage.

I stood, smoothing my skirt, and the people quieted.

King Valdren was next, leaping onto to the stage as if it were a small boulder, and then stood beside me. Piper watched us quietly from the front row.

"Bow before your queen!" he bellowed, smoke rising from his nostrils.

Every single head dipped and I swallowed hard, looking out over all of those heads bowed in fear. It was never the way I wanted to lead, and yet they didn't respond to reasonable actions, which was evident after Lucien had apologized. I peered over my shoulder at Mateo, who appeared relieved and also afraid at the sight of me.

"Are you the one who gave orders to free me?" he asked.

I nodded.

His brows pinched together. "And also the one that killed my brother?"

There was some genuine anger there, which told me that whatever had transpired with his brother he still had loved him. I could respect that.

Family was family.

"I am." I thought it best I took the blame for killing Marcelle since Lucien had enough of a stain on his reputation with the people of Summer.

"Kill her!" someone from the crowd screamed.

"Fake queen," another said.

Fear seized my chest at the thought that I might have to fight my way out of here. I wasn't scared of getting hurt but I didn't want to hurt anyone else in my flight to freedom. These were innocent, misled people.

"Touch me and I will suck the air from your lungs!" I bellowed to the crowd. I could not look weak now. There was no turning back.

"I could boil your blood without a touch," Mateo said behind me, to which the crowd roared their agreement.

Oh fae. This was not going well.

The *schling* of a blade leaving its scabbard had the

crowd going silent and all of us looked at the dragon king. "*Not* before I take your head," King Valdren said to Prince Mateo, holding his sword out and pointing the tip at him.

Mateo chuckled, as if he found this all amusing, and I wondered if his years away in captivity had hampered his ability to have diplomatic conversations. Mateo reached out his hand to me. "I am in your debt, Queen Madelynn. I do not like that my brother had to die for my freedom to come to pass, but I am rather grateful to be free."

So he was a little mad, maybe playing a game just now. A sigh of relief whooshed out of me and I reached out and shook his hand. King Valdren stayed close, sword at the ready.

The crowd booed and I turned on them. "Do we have a betrothed couple here? Speak up if you are betrothed!" I screamed at them.

Everyone looked around confused, wondering what I was playing at, and a girl stepped forward with a young man. "We are betrothed. So what?"

I nodded, pointing to the man. "He's mine now. You're dowry is canceled and I will marry him today," I told them.

The crowd gasped and the girl scowled at me.

"*That* is what Marcelle did to me! He canceled the agreement my father made with King Thorne. He threatened to kill my mother and sister if I didn't marry him and become your queen."

Gasps rang out, and I knew I was getting somewhere with them.

"So are you really surprised when Lucien caused another freeze on your land in an effort to get me back? Are you really shocked I killed the man who stole my innocence and forced me into marriage after I had already been promised?"

A dead silence fell over the crowd but I pressed on.

"Listen, I know you have a past with King Thorne and that you hate him for the Great Freeze all those years ago. But he's apologized for it, he confessed publicly that he couldn't control his powers, so it's time to move on. People make mistakes," I pleaded to them. "Marcelle was a bad man and a horrible leader. The sooner you realize that, the sooner we can move forward with the current crisis in which we find ourselves."

Murmurs ripped throughout the space and I felt Mateo and King Valdren step up beside me.

"What crisis!?" someone yelled.

This was it. This moment would decide whether or not these people would live or die, whether we might win the war or not.

"War with the Nightfall queen has already begun. She attempted to kidnap my little sister and now has a thousand men at the Winter Court border coming this way." Gasps and shrieks ripped through the space, but I pressed on. "Winter Court is the only thing keeping her from taking *all* of Thorngate. We need you to join Fall and Spring Court, and fight with us!"

The room erupted into shouts of dissent and fear.

King Valdren stepped up front and his voice filled the entire space. "Three days!" he boomed, and everyone fell quiet. "By my estimation and experience, three days is all you have before Queen Zaphira and her enhanced army make it here and kill you with your own powers."

Gasps, shock, and crying. It broke my heart to see such a naïve people come to terms with reality. But come to terms they must, or they would die.

I peered at Mateo. He was seen as an extension of Marcelle. They needed to hear from him.

He looked scared, his boyish face highlighting what little experience he had on these matters, but he nodded to me. "I will not force you to fight!" Mateo said to them and I winced.

I would have.

"I will go to the battlefield and represent Summer Court, and if you choose to stay back like a coward, and your children die at the hand of the Nightfall queen's men when they raid our beautiful home within three days' time, then I will *not* offer condolences," he bellowed.

Chills raced up my arms and the crowd erupted into shouts of agreement.

Mateo then looked to me. "I would like to formally reunite with Thorngate and cancel the separation my brother started."

Relief spread throughout my limbs.

"The elders agree! The fae will fight as one!" an older male fae in the crowd shouted.

I tipped my chin in agreement. "We will get that paperwork started just as soon as I can, but until then, meet me in Winter Court with your strongest warriors."

Mateo saluted me. "Prepare for war!" he shouted the command, and the people were thrown into action.

King Valdren pulled Mateo aside to the back of the stage where it was more private, and I followed them. Seeing the giant dragon king next to the small boy was almost comical.

"Have you ever led a battle?" the dragon king asked him.

The boy looked like he might be sick. "No, sir."

Valdren nodded. "Let your senior-most guard give suggestions and take the lead. The best thing you can do is be decisive. Indecision usually costs lives."

Mateo nodded but looked terrified.

"Once you get to Winter Court, King Thorne will command your men. You shouldn't encounter any issues before that," I told him.

Again he looked nervous, but inclined his head in understanding.

There. I'd done it. I'd gotten all of the fae back together under one cause. I turned to the dragon king then. "It's time to get revenge for my sister," I growled. I wanted to slap the Nightfall queen's men with a windstorm so powerful that they flew across the realm.

Drae dipped his chin in understanding, then we wished Mateo luck before grabbing Piper and heading out.

Thoughts of how closely my little sister came to being hurt, or her power being stripped away from her by one of the Nightfall queen's machines, made me seethe with anger. I felt a darkness inside of my power then, one I'd never experienced before. It was like if I didn't keep it in check, it would consume the entire realm. This must be what Lucien battled with every time his father struck him or he got angry.

Maker have mercy on any soul who tried to take my little sister and get away with it. The Nightfall queen would pay.

17

Drae flew us past the Winter palace and up and over Ice Mountain, where Vincent was currently drinking his life away. Finally, he lowered us into an open field, and the second he did I knew something was wrong. People were shouting orders and running around screaming. I looked out onto the battlefield, hoping to see the ice and snow wall that Lucien had built to fend off the Nightfall queen and her men, but all I saw was blood and death.

Peering over to a group of tents where women were

tending to a fire and boiling water, I motioned to it. "Go over there and stay safe," I told Piper.

She reached out and gave me a hug and then leapt out of the basket. I followed her. I wanted to pet the scales of the dragon king's neck like I would a dog and thank him for his help, but I knew that was probably inappropriate. There was no time for thank yous, because a man ran past me screaming at the top of his lungs. He was missing an arm and bleeding out as he bolted for the healers' tent. How were we losing? Why wasn't it very cold? Or snowing?

A stone sank in my gut. Was Lucien hurt?

I stood there in shock, trying to process what was happening, when Queen Kailani suddenly swam into view. She held a dagger, had soot on her fingers, and smelled oddly of... moonshine.

"What's happening?" I asked.

She gave me a grim expression. "Lucien's powers... barely work. The blood transfer weakened him considerably. We didn't know that before you left."

The world around me tilted then, causing dizziness to wash over me. Lucien saved my life, and in return I took his power? He'd never forgive me. Panic surged inside of me as I thought of our people out there getting slaughtered while Lucien couldn't protect them.

A group of Nightfall soldiers advanced towards us then and Kailani reached down into a bag she had laid at her feet. Coming up with a moonshine bottle, she lit the little strip of cloth hanging out of the opening. It flared to life with fire and she chucked it at the oncoming men. When it crashed to the ground at their feet, it exploded, causing me to jump backwards with a yelp. The men retreated, some of them on fire, and Kailani readied another moonshine bomb.

Holy fae. This was war.

I peered out into the chaos looking for Lucien and found him. He was out in the battlefield with his men, throwing small little bursts of snow and ice at an advancing group of Nightfall warriors.

I didn't think, I just ran. Guilt swirled inside of me as I thought about how he must be feeling. When Marcelle had cuffed me and I'd been without my power, I'd felt dead inside. I imagined he was going through the same thing. To be drained of power right before a war... it was a death sentence.

It was as if he sensed me. He turned, and when his gaze fell on me he dropped the sword he held and I leapt into his arms. A whimper ripped from his chest as his hands came up to grasp the sides of my face. "You're alive," he breathed.

Tears fell on my cheeks as war raged around us. I didn't even know what to say.

I was about to start trying to form some kind of apology for stealing his power when someone yanked me from behind. I spun, preparing to fight, and came face to face with a beautiful white-haired queen wearing the Embergate crest on her breastplate. She was covered in blood and held a large hunting blade and a wild expression.

I knew who this was... *Arwen Valdren*, the dragon king's wife.

"Are you the one who has the winter king's magic now?" she asked, looking from Lucien to me.

I swallowed hard and gave her a nod.

"Thank the Maker you are finally here!" she said and began to pull me backwards, towards where her husband was still in dragon form. Lucien followed, leaving the frontlines and jogging after us.

I was so lost in this moment I just let her pull me around because with every second I was starting to feel like everyone here was going to die and Lucien was never going to forgive me.

I took his power.

When we got to the dragon king, Arwen looked me deep in the eyes. "I would *kill* for my little sister. How about you?"

I swallowed hard, sobered by her serious question. I gave her a curt nod and she looked at the saddle on her husband's back. "Those bastards tried to take your kin and they've been killing our men all day. Remember that now and make them *hurt*."

I was so shocked by what she said that I just allowed her to shove me into the saddle. Lucien suddenly jumped in next to me and then Drae took off to the skies with a violent jerk.

"What's happening?" I asked him, peering down at the ground as Arwen grew smaller. "Why are we flying again?" I didn't want to leave, I wanted to help. I'd never met the dragon queen before, but it looked like she'd been fighting alongside our people all day and I respected the Hades out of her for it.

Lucien looked battle worn and weary. His was covered in snow and blood. Hopefully not his own. "You have to build the ice wall. We need time to regroup," he said quickly. "Are the other courts coming?"

I was still in shock at this turn of events, but I nodded. "They are."

Lucien grasped my hands and took them in his. "Madelynn, look at me."

I turned and met his gaze. "You *have* to save our people. I need you to call on the winter power you hold and build an ice wall as tall as a building."

Panic spiraled inside of my chest. "Lucien, I don't know how. I have made just a single ice shard—"

His hands dropped mine and then gripped the side of my face. "You can do this. I will help you. We *have* to try. They're slaughtering us."

Seeing into his swimming gray eyes, I was wracked with guilt. If his people died because I stole his power, I would never forgive myself.

"Okay, tell me what to do." I shook out my hands as he let go of my face, then I peered over the side of the dragon king. There was a line of bodies all along the border between Nightfall and Thorngate. Snow flurried everywhere as his men fought, but bursts of flames melted their hard work. The queen's men had Summer Court power, among others, as I saw a small wind tunnel blow over one man.

Lucien leaned into me, pressing his mouth against my ear. "The trick with winter is that it's unforgiving, brutal, and cares little for life."

Okay, a dark start, but I was trying to take inspiration from that.

"The single emotion that controls winter magic... is anger," he said.

I looked over at him, surprised to hear him admit such a thing, and he nodded.

It made sense then, why he was so powerful. Every time his father struck him or verbally cut him down, Lucien just stored up more fuel for his power. It also made sense with what I'd felt so far from this winter magic I held. It was volatile, like anger.

His breath was warm across my neck. "Think of the single most infuriating thing that's ever happened to you and channel it through the winter power." He pointed to the demarcation line between the two realms, a small dotting of rocks and melting snow. "Then aim it there," he added.

The dragon king was hovering over the spot I needed to concentrate my power, so I took a deep breath in, afraid to go into what my most infuriating memory even was. I thought of my father selling me to Marcelle after promising me to Lucien, but deep down I loved my father and so it didn't hold enough anger. I then went to Marcelle forcing me to marry him in the carriage, and that fueled the fire inside of me, but not enough.

It was in the memory of Marcelle taking my purity that ignited a bomb. I hadn't truly allowed myself to process that trauma and all it meant to me. I'd been living in survival mode since the moment Marcelle kidnapped me from my father's study.

I allowed everything he'd done to me to come to the forefront of my mind and the anger exploded in my chest. A scream ripped from my throat and tears slid down my cheeks as I remembered the violent way in which Marcelle took what I'd saved for Lucien.

Flinging my hands over the basket, I threw a torrent of wind, ice, and snow onto the battlefield.

Lucien's hand slipped over my thigh and squeezed

as if he knew all too well what it was like to hold this anger.

The temperature in the air around us plunged to frigid depths and my teeth chattered, but I kept on. I pushed on the power and fused it with my anger, creating a storm of epic proportions. Slowly but surely, a wall of ice built on the ground. I could see it, like a barrier of growing glass, and I could feel it in the tips of my fingers. It was hard to explain. The troops had to break up and run back to their respective sides as the wall got higher and higher. At the same time, the snow and wind blew at the Nightfall army, pushing them to retreat to the safety of their realm.

"That's it, keep feeding the power," Lucien coaxed.

His father flashed into my mind. A man I barely knew, and yet it angered me that he'd refused to get help for his condition. That he'd chosen a bottle over his own son.

With a growl of frustration, I threw as much magic as possible and Lucien gasped as the wall of ice suddenly shot forty feet into the air.

Drae flew backwards to avoid being hit by it and I finally let go of the anger I'd held onto.

"You did it," Lucien breathed.

Cheers sounded from the battlefield below and the dragon king started his descent. Lucien pulled my hand into his lap and stroked small circles into it.

I grinned, peering down at the giant ice wall, and then over at Lucien. I wasn't prepared for his frown and downcast gaze. "What's wrong?" I asked over the sound of the wind.

"I am of no use to you or my people now that I don't have my power." His admission filled the entire space, saying everything unsaid.

No longer caring for propriety, I took his face in my hands and pressed my lips to his. I ached for him to know how much he meant to me, how fond of him I'd grown in such a short time. How everything he perceived as a flaw was what I loved most about him.

Pulling back from his mouth, I looked him in the eyes. "Lucien Thorne, you will *never* be useless to me."

There was a fire in his eyes, one lit by passion, one that I knew could only be quenched by more kisses.

When we landed, a messenger rode our way. "The Nightfall army retreats!" he shouted, and everyone cheered, hoisting their fists into the air.

"She'll be back tomorrow with more men and more anger," Lucien said to me.

"Then let's make the most of tonight." I kissed his neck, feeling his quickening pulse beneath my lips. "Marry me before this war gets too big."

"Yes, sugar plum." He leaned forward and kissed my nose.

WITHIN HOURS, we were ready for a wedding. I had no white dress, there was not enough fancy food, we had no band, and neither the cathedral nor the ballroom could hold all of the fae and elves and dragon-folk present, but it was perfect. Spring, Summer, and Fall had all arrived moments ago, ready to fight for King Thorne and I. The elves and dragon-folk had heard of the war brewing at the ice wall and made their way too, and that's how we had over six thousand warriors at our wedding.

We'd long ago ditched the ballroom idea. The garden was out too because of the size. The beautiful cathedral his mother had built wouldn't cut it either. Instead we opted for the town square. It was filled to the brim with warriors and families. Tents were erected to smoke meat and make beans with rice to feed everyone. It was not the wedding that I had envisioned as a little girl, and yet somehow it was more than I imagined. After all of the pain that the separation caused, our people had finally come together. United.

The priest handed me the single candlestick, fire flickering as I touched it to Lucien's, igniting his flame. Together we touched them both to the larger candle, and when it was lit, we blew ours out.

"Two lives become one today," the priest said to

everyone gathered as Lucien and I stood on a makeshift stage in the center of town. "Two leaders with a shared love of our people." He then looked to me.

All fae weddings were sealed with the same poem. It was written so long ago no one knew who penned the words, but it encompassed all of us so beautifully that we recited it each wedding to declare our intentions. I memorized it when I was five.

"For as surely as snow melts into water, and as wind moves a flickering flame, my love for you is true and will never fade," I said to Lucien.

Lucien held my gaze, never wavering. "For as surely as snow melts into water, and as wind moves a flickering flame, my love for you is true and will never fade," he repeated.

The crowd erupted into applause and Lucien looked to the priest, who nodded. One second Lucien was a foot away from me, and the next our bodies were crushed together, his lips on mine as the gathered people went wild.

I grinned against his mouth as his tongue teased at my lips. I opened them and stroked my tongue against his.

This kiss was *so* inappropriate, my mother was probably having heart failure. But I didn't care. Only when the priest cleared his throat did we both pull away, beaming.

Lucien then stepped up to the edge of the stage and slipped his hand into mine, raising it above our heads.

Everyone quieted and then Lucien dropped our hands to a more relaxed gesture at his side.

"On the brink of war, Madelynn and I would like to give our people a future to look forward to!" he announced, and people cheered.

Lucien gazed at me and I knew he was wrestling with a heavy topic.

"I never publicly apologized for the Great Freeze that affected so many lives all those years ago and I would like to do so now. That night, my father had too much to drink and was... unkind to me." Our people gasped, reaching up to cover their mouths, but Lucien went on. "I lost control of my powers. The grief and rage of losing my mother, along with my father's abuse, was too much for me to bear that night and I snapped."

The crowd gasped again and I squeezed Lucien's hand tightly in support. I'd never been prouder of him in this moment, as a man, a husband, and a king. Being vulnerable and taking responsibility for his actions was not easy, but he had done it, and his people would love him for it.

"I used to think speaking of such things would be seen as a weakness, but I no longer care. I want you all to know that from the bottom of my heart, I made a mistake and I am sorry." He dipped his head in shame then and I looked out at the gathered crowd. There wasn't a dry eye to be seen. Even the dragon-folk and elves looked misty-eyed.

People began to rush the stage then and I panicked for a moment, wondering what was happening. Lucien's guards sprinted forward but it was too late, I was yanked from where I stood and Lucien went with me.

"Long live the king and queen!" Cheers rang out as we were hoisted into the air by our people.

I gazed at Lucien in wonder and he reached for my hand, raising it into the air with a grin. We were on our backs, looking up into the sky as our people supported our weight and carried us over the crowd of thousands.

This went on for almost half an hour. We were carried around the entire town square by Spring, Fall, Summer, and Winter Court fae. I'd never seen our people this intermingled and together. It was in this moment that I realized that our wedding was exactly what was needed during this time of strife.

After that, we sat humbly on some shop steps with our people eating a basic meal of beans and rice and some steamed meat. People laughed and danced to the sounds of fiddles and told stories of times long past.

Piper came to find us when the moon was high in

the sky. "I'm sorry, I need the newly married couple," she told the group of courtiers we were chatting with.

They nodded and wished us farewell, and we followed her through the crowd. My mother blew me a kiss as I passed and I caught it in the air. Libby was asleep on a blanket at her feet.

When we reached the edge of the main town square, Piper stopped in front of a horse and turned to me. "Go have some time alone. Tomorrow the war really begins," she told us.

She'd guarded my purity her whole life, and now she was pushing me to bed my husband. I totally approved.

Lucien clasped his hands together in gratitude. "You are perfection," he told Piper, causing her to grin.

We both practically leapt onto the horse and rode it back to Winter Castle. When we reached there, one of his attendants was waiting to take the stallion from him.

Lucien casually guided me inside and back to his side of the castle. I'd never been to his room, and with each step we took I was reminded that the purity I had intended to save for him... was gone.

When we reached the large oak door, Lucien opened it and we stepped inside. I was taken by how light and bright everything was. I'd expected black and grays but it was all cream and white.

Snow. It reminded me of snow. His couch, bed, drapes, wall color, it was all white or varying shades of cream, which brightened the entire space.

Turning, Lucien grasped my face in his hands. "We have the rest of our lives together. If you're not ready—"

My lips crashed into his and I was rewarded with a moan.

I thought after my traumatic situation with Marcelle, I might never want to bed anyone again. But it was the opposite. I craved this moment with Lucien so that it could replace the awful one Marcelle had stolen. I wanted to show my body that it was safe to love this man and he would not betray us. I wanted to imprint a new memory in my body, filled with love and tenderness.

All of our past kisses had been somewhat public or out in the open, but this kiss, sequestered in the privacy of our now shared bedroom, was carefree, raw and carnal in nature. Lucien tangled his fingers in my hair, pulling it lightly as I clawed at his chest. Our tongues stroked against each other softly as I pressed my hips into him. Pulling back from me, Lucien gave me a wild look, and there was something animalistic in his gaze.

"Last chance to back out," he breathed, and I could see the pulse pounding in his neck.

"I'm all in," I assured him, panting.

It was as if I'd let a wild animal out of a cage. His hands came up behind me and tore at the laces of my dress, ripping them to expose my breasts. I gasped and then did the same to him, yanking at his tunic until he pulled it over his head. Within seconds we were both naked and staring at each other.

His eyes drank in every inch of my bare skin, and I didn't cross my arms over my chest to hide, or push my thighs together. I stood there boldly, displaying my body as I took him in as well.

Lucien Thorne was a masterpiece. If I were a sculptor, I would carve his body from rock, paying careful attention to the knotted abdominal muscles and the V-shape at his pelvis.

"You own me," Lucien breathed, stepping closer to me until our bodies were touching. "Every part of my body and soul is yours, Madelynn Windstrong," he whispered as he picked me up and set me on the bed. I gasped at the way his declaration rolled around my heart, and then I moaned when his lips made contact with my breast.

My back arched as pleasure and heat bloomed between my legs, and then Lucien was there, his hand making circles at my most sensitive spot.

My entire life I was taught to be perfect, to hold back any sexual thoughts or actions, act proper, keep pure. And in this moment, in the safety of my marital bed, with the man I loved, I let loose.

Grinding into his hand, I panted as Lucien dragged his tongue across my neck.

"I need you," I moaned.

A second later he was there, lying next to me, grabbing my hips and pulling me on top of him.

I was worried I wouldn't know what to do, that I should have probably asked a few married friends how to make this work and feel good for both of us. But, to my relief, Lucien and my lovemaking was as easy and carefree as when we did magic together.

My wind, his snow.

We fit perfectly, dancing together with the flow of our bodies, chasing pleasure and riding waves of bliss until we both collapsed on the bed panting.

When Lucien turned to look at me, he shook his head.

"What?" I grew concerned.

"I can't believe you threatened to only bed me for making children," he scoffed. "I would die under such conditions."

I tipped my head back and laughed deep in my belly as he popped up on one elbow and gazed at my naked form.

"War and death and seriousness comes tomorrow," he said somberly.

I nodded, pulling his hand over to cup my breast. "But we will always have tonight."

And we did. We lay together three times and built a night of memories and lovemaking to last deep into the depression of war that would surely come for us as we banded together to take on the Nightfall queen.

Lucien let me sleep in! I felt a bit silly as I stepped into the dining hall for breakfast to see it full of kings and queens of nearly all the magical races.

Queen Kailani greeted me with a hug. "Epic wedding."

Arwen nodded. "Way more fun than ours." She looked to her husband.

He winced. "I had too much mead."

I stepped closer to Arwen. "I'm Madelynn, I don't think we've been *officially* introduced," I told the dragon queen. She'd helped so much with the war and had taken charge when I was in shock, but I'd barely spoken a word to her. She was at the wedding, but off in the distance. There had been too many people and we hadn't had a chance to get to know each other.

Arwen grinned. "The woman who thawed the winter king's heart? I love you already." She rushed forward and pulled me into hug. Laughter erupted from my chest and I hugged her back. When we pulled away, Lucien was there with a smile as he placed a kiss on my cheek.

"Morning," he whispered.

I looked at the scene before me and tucked into breakfast. There was a war map of the realm with figurines smack dab in the middle of the table. Bowls and platters of food sat around the edges of the map, and everyone grabbed fruit and breads and meat as they all shouted random ideas. I expected the other wives to complain about having a war map on the dining table but they were pointing out weaknesses in the border and advantages. I realized that they too were not just decorations. These were warrior women I sat with, and was proud to host in our home.

Arwen's twin girls were brought in and out of the room by their nursemaids, and it was so sweet to see the dragon king dote on them. He kissed their faces, their feet, and rubbed their little hands along his scruffy beard.

As Lucien and Raife were arguing over the Narrow Strait, a messenger came into the dining hall with a wounded warrior. The Winter Soldier was missing an arm. It was wrapped tightly in gauze with a tourniquet.

Lucien stood quickly and rushed to the man's side. "Ardell," Lucien greeted the soldier.

King Lightstone stood as well and went to the man's side. "Do you need healing?"

Ardell shook his head. "Bleeding has stopped. Unless you can grow back an arm?"

King Lightstone frowned. "I cannot."

Ardell nodded. "I bring news, my lord. Distressing news." He looked at everyone in the room.

"Speak freely, these are my closest friends and allies," Lucien told him.

Ardell took in a shuddering breath. "I've snuck into Nightfall like you asked. I spied on the queen's soldiers for a full day before I was caught and then got free."

We all steeled ourselves for the next thing he was going to say.

"What did you see?" Lucien placed a comforting hand on his good shoulder.

Ardell looked off at the far wall as if reliving a trauma. "Her men... some of them... they can shift forms like the wolves at Fallenmoore."

I gasped, standing from my chair and walking closer to him to make sure I'd heard him correctly.

"What do you mean?" Lucien spoke slowly. "They've been bitten? They're changed?"

Ardell shook his head. "They're not as big as Fallenmoore wolves. And some of them can only partially shift, but it's enough to do damage." He held up his bloody stump of an arm for effect.

Lucien began to pace the dining hall as the elf king reached out and held his hand over the man's wound. A purple light emanated from his palm and the man's face relaxed. "Thank you, my lord."

"Is there anything else you can tell us?" King Lightstone asked him.

Ardell inclined his head. "They have hundreds of the machines they use to strip us of power. They're on wheels, and a person only need lie in it for a few moments before their power is sucked into an elixir."

"An elixir!" Queen Kailani stood, and so did the dragon king and queen. It seemed no one could sit any longer. We'd collectively lost our appetite.

Ardell nodded. "The soldier drinks the elixir and then has the magical power."

King Lightstone and Queen Kailani shared a look. "We must have missed that," they said in unison.

I didn't know what they were talking about. My mind was stuck on the fact that Nightfall soldiers, against all odds, were now imbued with every creature's power in Avalier.

"Thank you, Ardell. You may retire from service. You will receive full soldier's benefits for the rest of your life," Lucien told him.

Ardell dipped his chin. "Permission to stay on and fight? My magic still works with one arm."

Lucien grinned. "Permission granted. Go rest up."

Ardell bowed to all of us and left, and then the room exploded into dialog.

"They have the power of wolves now!"

"How long has she had these machines!?"

"An elixir!"

"I need her head on a spike!"

Lucien whistled and the room quieted. Everyone turned to him and he spoke calmly but directly. "Between Embergate and our lands, we have Zaphira surrounded," Lucien said, pointing to the map. "But we need to get word to Axil. He's reclusive, and only ever bothered with his own kind. I doubt he knows she's been stealing his people's power and that war is afoot."

King Lightstone nodded. "He's always been closer with you. Could you go to him, since your power isn't working?"

The room was plunged into a frigid chill suddenly and our breath came out in a fog.

"Actually, it's back full bore. I tried early this morning," he said with a grin. I smiled at Lucien, incredibly happy for him.

Queen Arwen rubbed her hands up her arms. "Okay, no need to show off," she teased.

"Sorry," Lucien muttered, and the temperature raised again.

I felt such relief that his power was fully back I nearly collapsed into my seat. A thought struck me then. "I can go," I blurted out. "The war has begun and Lucien is powerful. He needs to stay here and protect our people."

"No way," Lucien said quickly.

Kailani cleared her throat. "Actually... maybe we could do a girls' trip kind of idea. Queen Arwen will fly Queen Madelynn and me. That way, you men can hold down the front while we are gone. We can bring back Axil and his army."

A girls' trip to find the wolf king? I quite liked that idea, and from the grin on Kailani's face, she did too.

"With all due respect, my love," King Lightstone looked at his wife, "I'm not sending you into Fallenmoore unprotected."

Kailani scowled at her husband. "I don't need a guard! I can steal a person's life with one breath," she snapped, and the elf king fell silent.

Whoa, I had heard she was powerful, but her magic was slightly unknown. It was all rumors. She brought back the dead, she sucked a person's soul from their body, she could read your mind. Rumors circled over the past few weeks, making it all the way to Fall Court that she'd singlehandedly run off the Nightfall queen with the elvin army while her husband was out of town. I didn't know how much of it was true though.

"So can I," I told her, and she shot me a grin.

The dragon king opened his mouth to speak, and Arwen put up a hand to stop him. "Don't even bother. I'm going. I'll be back in two days' time. The girls have a wet nurse. They will be fine."

Drae's mouth clamped shut and his jaw grit, but he said nothing.

"So it's settled," I said. "We will go and get Axil and bring his wolves back to the front and finish off Zaphira."

The men all shared a look, one that said they wished they could speak alone but knew they couldn't.

"Flying to Fallenmoore is safer than being here right now," Lucien offered the other kings.

Drae let out a relenting sigh. "But when have you last heard from Axil?"

"He sent a letter last spring," Lucien said. "It was generic: he was having issues with his brother, and would be taking a wife soon."

"Do we even know if he would help?" the dragon king doubled down. "The wolves are so secluded. They don't like to bother with outsiders' problems."

The elf king nodded. "But we now have proof

Zaphira is taking his people's power. That's a wolf problem."

Lucien cleared his throat. "Axil has never met our wives. What will make him believe they really come with our wishes and can act with our authority?"

The dragon and elf king both shared a mischievous grin, then Drae walked to the door. "Be right back," he uttered mysteriously.

He returned a moment later holding a small box. It was metal and the corners were rusted. Drae brushed it off and held it up for Lucien to inspect.

Lucien's entire face fell, and he went a little pale. "You dug it up," he breathed, his voice full of emotion.

"I did," Drae said, and brought it to the dining table.

Arwen slipped her hand into Drae's as Kailani walked over to be held by Raife, and I moved towards Lucien.

"What is it?" I asked, clearly the only one who didn't know.

Lucien looked at me, his eyes misty. "A memory box. We were eight or nine years old and we all buried something—Raife, Drae, Axil, and I."

That was so sweet. We could bring the box and Axil would for sure believe that we were the wives of these kings.

Kailani peered forward to look at the box. "So are you going to open it?"

Drae glanced at Lucien. "Raife and I were going to bring it to you to open."

Lucien sighed, looking slightly sad. "Let's wait for Axil. We'll open it all together after we win the war."

My heart sank a little. I was sort of dying to know what nine-year-old Lucien buried as a memory. But from the look on his face, he wasn't ready to dig that up.

There was a knock at the door and Piper peeked her head inside. "Can I speak to you for a moment?" she asked me, and I nodded, excusing myself while they planned our trip up north.

When I closed the door behind me, Piper walked down the hall quickly, and I ran to catch up. "What's up?" I asked her.

She turned the corner into the library and I followed, coming face to face with Lucien's father.

I recoiled at the stench of urine and wine. Lucien's father stood there with red-rimmed eyes and a shaking foot. He was in quite a state, and I shared a nervous look with Piper, who stayed beside me for moral support.

Vincent peered at Piper, and when she didn't leave he cleared his throat. "I missed the wedding," he said to me.

That's what this was about? "You did," I told him, wondering why he was here. He knew my rule.

His hands balled into fists as he seemed to be at a loss for words. "I was never a great father... but maybe I could be a decent grandfather? I... want to get better," he finally said, and my heart grew wings. "I haven't had a drink in twenty-four hours and I'm ready to go to that elvin healing place you mentioned."

I sighed in relief, and even though I was still mad at him for all of the abuse he'd dished out on Lucien, I pulled him into a hug. The moment my arms went around him, he stiffened as if he'd never been hugged in his life.

Then he relaxed, his arms coming around me as sobs wracked his body.

Piper slipped out of the room then and I knew without asking that she was readying a carriage to take him to the elvin treatment center for healing, which I hoped would one day also heal my husband and the part of him that probably, deep down, still loved this mess of a man.

When we finally pulled away, I knew I probably had his stink on me.

He wiped at his eyes. "Sorry about that. What an idiot I am," he muttered.

I frowned, wondering who taught him to talk about

himself like that. Probably *his* father. "I look forward to seeing you sober, Vincent."

He nodded. "I'm... scared. It's only been one day without the wine and I'm feeling things I don't want to feel."

"I think that's normal," I told him, but really I couldn't imagine what it was like to be scared to feel your own feelings. I wasn't him.

I didn't realize Lucien was behind me in the open doorway until he spoke. "Your carriage is ready, Father." His voice was clipped and I froze.

Vincent glanced at his son and wiped the last remnant of a tear from his face. He gave me a curt nod and then walked past me, stopping in the doorway to look up at his son, who was a few inches taller than him. "Your mom would be proud of the man you have become. A much better one than me." His dad reached up and lightly cupped his cheek. "I'm sorry," he whispered, and then walked out of the room.

I stood there frozen, unsure what to do to support Lucien in this moment.

"Holy fae," Lucien said, and I stared at him wide-eyed.

"What?" I asked.

"I didn't know he knew the words 'I'm sorry' existed," he joked.

I relaxed a little, knowing we were going the joking

route with this. Stepping over to him, I grasped the place his father had touched on his cheek. "He's right. You are a better man than him, and nothing like him." I kissed his lips and was rewarded with a smile, which turned to a wince.

"You stink, sugar plum." Lucien looked down at my dress.

"I'll go change for the journey." I chuckled.

For the first time in my life, I was wearing... pants. Arwen had convinced Kailani and I that it would be easier to ride in and move through Fallenmoore on foot if needed. To be honest, I was mortified to be seen in such things, but they were also really roomy and comfortable. And they had pockets!

"I can make my way to you in a half a day," Drae said to his wife as Kailani and Raife were a few feet over, having their own goodbye. We had water, food, maps and the tin box.

Lucien pulled me aside and looked down at me with a gaze that told me his heart was breaking just as much as mine.

We *just* got married. I'd slept in his arms one night. It wasn't enough. I wanted more.

His eyes were wide and full of trepidation. "I only just got you. I'm not ready to let you go."

"I will bring back King Axil and his men and we will win this war. I promise." I threaded my fingers into his and then leaned forward to place a kiss on his lips. He was hesitant at first, but then he opened his mouth and deepened the kiss.

When I pulled away, he smiled as he ran his fingers through my hair. "I don't know what's worse, not knowing what you taste like, or knowing and then not being able to kiss you."

I grinned. "Definitely the latter."

He swallowed hard. "If anything happens to you, I'll freeze this entire realm. I won't be able to control it."

Fear spiked in my heart because I knew he was telling the truth. "I'll be fine. Please keep my family safe."

He nodded. "Of course."

"Alright, lovebirds! We gotta fly," Kailani called out from behind Lucien. Arwen had shifted into a beautiful blue dragon and the elf queen was loading supplies into her basket.

There was nothing more to say. We'd said all of our goodbyes, had our kisses. The only thing to do was to leave the ones we loved and go flying into unknown danger for the good of our people. Such was the way of a queen.

Lucien helped lift me into the basket on Arwen's back and I settled into the seat with Kailani. "Do you plan on needing those?" I asked her as I took in the small open box of alcohol bottles. The tops were open and there were strips of soaked cloth hanging out the top.

Kailani grinned. "Backup plan in case anyone messes with us on the way."

I liked her, really liked her. She was unlike any lady I'd ever met. Piper and my mom and Libby came running out to wave us off then, and I tried not to look at the tears on my sister's cheeks.

As Arwen kicked off the ground, I swallowed my emotions down and put on a smile, waving to everyone.

Once we were up in the air, Kailani grabbed the tin box and shook it lightly, rattling the contents. "Are we going to peek?" she asked me with a devilish grin.

I laughed and took the box from her, setting it by our feet. "No, let's give it to King Axil as promised."

Kailani pouted but settled into the seat for the flight. It started to snow then, a fine dusting covering us as we left Winter Court.

"Awww," Kailani said. "He made it snow for you."

I turned and looked down at the ground. Everyone else had gone inside but Lucien. He was staring up at us as snow fell from the sky.

It reminded me of the day he came to negotiate my dowry, how he'd given in to everything I wanted and heaped compliments on me and respected our household staff.

Lucien Thorne had been nothing like I imagined. He was so much better, and I prayed to the Maker that we'd win this war and get to live the rest of our lives together.

———

THE FLIGHT over Archmere and into Fallenmoore was breathtaking. I'd been to Archmere once but never from this vantage point. It was *so* green. It looked like Spring and parts of Fall, but all over. Then when we got to the border of Fallenmoore I was grateful for my fur cloak. It reminded me of Winter Court and Lucien. Snowcapped mountains spanned the horizon for as far as the eye could see.

I'd never considered myself sheltered. I was a princess and had traveled all throughout Archmere and Embergate, but it wasn't until this moment, when I saw the pack of wolves down below, that I realized how little of the realm I had experienced.

I looked to Kailani, whose eyes were wide, and knew that she too had never seen a wolven.

"They're so big," I exclaimed, as Arwen lowered us to the ground.

The hulking mass of fur and muscle was a sight to behold.

They were larger than a cougarin and almost as big as a bearin! I suddenly felt nervous about the task ahead of us. Were they civil in their animal form? Or only as humans? I knew the moon affected them, and I'd heard them howling once when I visited a border town in Archmere. The wolves knew we were here, and craned their heads skyward as we descended over them.

Kailani reached down and clutched the tin box tightly as Arwen landed among the pack of two dozen or so wolves.

They circled us, surrounding Arwen on all sides as Kailani and I stepped out of the basket and approached one of the wolves.

The wolven was looking us right in the eyes, and

had cocked their head to the side, so I could see the intelligence there.

"My name is Queen Madelynn of Thorngate," I told them.

Kailani bowed slightly beside me and I kicked myself for not doing the same. "I am Queen Kailani of Archmere, and that is Queen Arwen of Embergate. We seek an audience with your king."

I watched the wolven who'd cocked her head as her face began to change. It looked like it was... melting. The sound of bones cracking filled the space as her fur retreated and gave way to smooth skin. It was horrifying and fascinating at the same time and I could not look away, even when the creature was reduced to a naked female who crouched in the dirt staring up at us.

I swallowed hard as she stood and tipped her chin high, meeting my gaze and never dropping it. She didn't say a word, she just held my gaze. I started to wonder if maybe they didn't speak Avalierian and had a mother tongue we didn't know, when she grinned.

"You are an alpha among your people?" she asked. Her long dark hair cascaded over one shoulder, but her breasts were exposed as well as the rest of her, and yet she made no effort to cover herself.

I had to remind myself that these were cultural customs that might be normal to them and so I tried to act like it didn't bother me. "I am," I told her. Alpha and queen were similar. We were both leaders of our people.

"Can you take us to King Moon?" Kailani asked.

The wolven woman pointed to the mountain range in the distance, where a small stream of fire curled towards the sky.

"Our king lives on Death Mountain. You will find him there," she said.

Death Mountain. That didn't sound too cozy.

"Thank you." I bowed my head and she hissed.

Walking over, she reached out and grasped my chin, tipping my head up. "*Don't* bow unless you are submissive. If you are an alpha, a queen, you keep your chin up, maintain eye contact. If the king thinks you are weak, he will kill you."

My eyes bugged at that moment. Kill me? I was a queen of a neighboring territory. Surely she didn't mean it?

Kailani and I shared a worried look, then the woman stared at Arwen's dragon form. "She is a threat to the king. She cannot go to Death Mountain in dragon form or she'll be shot from the sky without question. She stays here or walks there as a human."

Okay, clearly there were some rules here we hadn't known about. I started to panic, unsure now what to do. But before I could even think of a solution, Arwen shifted back into her human body.

More cracking bones, dragon scales turned to soft pink skin, and now I was standing before *two* naked women.

Good grief.

Trying to maintain eye contact when a woman's breasts were exposed was harder than I realized. I was trying to conceal my blush but knew I must be failing.

"They're not going anywhere without me," Arwen told the woman, holding her eye contact, chin held high like the wolven had suggested.

The dark-haired woman grinned. "Two alphas," she said through her smile.

Kailani scoffed. "*Three* alphas. I'm an alpha too."

The woman shook her head. "No. You're second-in-command. Maybe. More like mid-pack."

Kailani frowned at that and crossed her arms over her chest. It seemed the custom here was to size up a person and immediately rank them based on dominance. Little did she know Kailani was a powerful warrior.

Arwen cleared her throat. "Would you and your pack escort us to Death Mountain? We can pay you."

The woman looked at a wolf behind her and something unseen passed between them. "We will take you to the base of the mountain. We avoid politics whenever possible," she said.

That was an interesting comment.

Avoid politics... were they some rebel pack that lived outside of government rule?

"Thank you," Arwen said, and then began to rifle through her basket for clothes and shoes. Once she was bundled up, the wolven woman shifted back into her wolf form without a word. The pack broke up and about a dozen of the wolves formed a V, pointing the way, and we walked inside of it.

Once we'd been walking for about an hour, Arwen slipped closer to Kailani and I. "None of the other kings besides Lucien have spoken to Axil since they were young boys. We don't know what kind of situation we will be walking into here, but if anything goes wrong, get outside and I fly us home."

We nodded and I found myself wondering what could go wrong. Lucien had spoken to me of King Axil like a beloved friend. He told me they sent letters over the years and remained on good terms since their yearly retreats stopped.

"Lucien speaks highly of King Axil. Said he would not hesitate to help us," I told them in an attempt to put their minds at ease.

Kailani looked sideways at me. "Then why were we told Arwen would be shot out of the sky?"

I chewed my lip. Good point. Only the dragon king or queen could shift into a dragon. If he'd told his men to shoot a dragon out of the sky, he would be knowingly killing the king or queen.

I lowered my voice to barely a whisper, the loudest sound being the crunching of our boots on snow. "If need be, I can protect us with my wind power. We will be okay."

Arwen looked at me with unease. "Do you know the power the wolf king holds?"

I swallowed the lump of trepidation lodged in my throat at her tone. "He can shift into a very large wolf?"

Arwen chuckled. "The king of the wolves can take over your mind and render your wind power useless."

My mouth went bone dry. Take over my mind? But... "Are you sure?"

Arwen gazed at the lead wolf who we'd spoken with earlier. She was watching us and simply gave a single nod. Great, she'd heard our entire conversation.

"Yep," Arwen confirmed.

Oh fae. What had we gotten ourselves into?

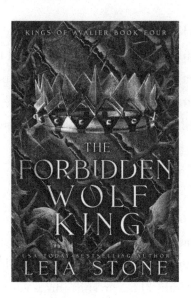

BOOK FOUR: The Forbidden Wolf is already on Presale on Amazon.

ACKNOWLEDGMENTS

Always a big thank you to my amazing readers! I truly could not do this without you. It still amazes me that I get to be creative and do this for a living and someone actually wants to read what I write. Thank you to my Wolf Pack who is so supportive. To my editors Lee and Kate, I am a sloppy mess without you. And always to my husband and children for sharing me with my art. <3

FOLLOW ME

Amazon:

I have over 50 fantasy books for you to enjoy! Check them out on amazon.

Wolf Pack:

Please join my Leia Stone Wolf Pack on Facebook as I often reveal covers and secret bookish things in there as well as doing giveaways.

Newsletter:

Also sign up for my Newsletter at LeiaStone.com so you don't miss a New Release. I don't spam and you can leave anytime.

Social Media:

Follow me on Instagram and Tik Tok and "Like" my Facebook page.

Made in the USA
Coppell, TX
07 May 2023

16547385R00199